THE GREAT PROFUNDO

Bernard Mac Laverty was born in Belfast, where he worked for ten years as a medical laboratory technician before studying English at Queen's University. He then moved to Scotland and taught for a number of years. He now writes full-time and lives in Glasgow.

He has written two novels, *Lamb* and *Cal*, both of which have been made into successful films, and four collections of short stories: *Secrets*, *A Time to Dance*, *The Great Profundo* and *Walking the Dog*. His new novel, *Grace Notes*, is published by Jonathan Cape.

Bernard Mac Laverty

THE GREAT
PROFUNDO

and Other Stories

For Tony

well met in Trieste

Bernard Mac Laverty

V

10.VII.99.

VINTAGE

Published by Vintage 1997

2 4 6 8 10 9 7 5 3 1

Copyright © Bernard Mac Laverty 1987

Versions of 'The Break' and 'Across the Street' first
appeared in the *Irish Times* Summer Stories, 1984 and
1985; 'More than just the Disease' in *Scottish Short Stories*, Collins, 1983; 'End of Season' in *Firebird 3*, Penguin,
1984; and 'Remote' in the *Sunday Tribune*, 22 December
1985

First published in Great Britain by
Jonathan Cape Ltd, 1987

Vintage
Random House, 20 Vauxhall Bridge Road, London SW1V 2SA

Random House Australia (Pty) Limited
20 Alfred Street, Milsons Point, Sydney
New South Wales 2061, Australia

Random House New Zealand Limited
18 Poland Road, Glenfield,
Auckland 10, New Zealand

Random House South Africa (Pty) Limited
Endulini, 5A Jubilee Road, Parktown 2193, South Africa

Random House UK Limited Reg. No. 954009

A CIP catalogue record for this book
is available from the British Library

ISBN 0 09 977371 6

For Ciara

Contents

Words the Happy Say

After he had cleared the breakfast things he guided the crumbs to the edge of the table with a damp cloth and wiped them into his cupped and withered hand. He took out his board and laid it on the cleaned surface. Some people liked to work at a tilt but he had always preferred it flat in front of him. From his back window on the third floor he could hear the children moving along the driveway into the primary school. Because it was summer and the large lime tree, sandwiched between the blackened gable ends, was in full leaf, he could see them only from the waist down. He noticed the boys with rumpled socks and dirty shoes always walked together. Girls, neat in white ankle-socks, would hop-scotch and skip past in a different group. If he stood on tiptoe at the window he could see down into the small backyard but he no longer bothered to get up from his work for the diversion of seeing the new girl downstairs getting a shovel of coal.

He arranged his inks and distilled water and set his porcelain mixing-dish in the middle. Each shallow oval indentation shone with a miniature reflection of the window. He looked at the page he had been working on the previous day and his mouth puckered in distaste. He was unhappy that he had started the thing in English Roundhand and thought of going back again and beginning in Chancery.

'We, the Management and Staff of V.R. Wilson & Sons Bakery Ltd, wish to offer our heartfelt thanks and sincere gratitude to MR VERNON WILSON for all he has done in the forty-two years he has been head of V.R. WILSON & SONS BAKERY LTD . . . '

He worked quietly for an hour getting the Indian ink part finished, listening to the soft, pulled scratch of the pen, forming each letter in a perfect flow of black and at the perfect angle. He was always impatient to rub out the horizontal pencil guide-lines but took the precaution of making and drinking a cup of coffee before he did so. A page could be ruined that way. The rubber across damp ink could make a crow's wing of a down-stroke. He settled to drawing in pencil the embellish-ments to the opening W, then painted a lemon surround with tendrils of vermilion. He had to paint quickly and surely to avoid patchiness — a double layer of colour.

Suddenly he lifted his head and listened. There was a hesitant knock on the lower door. He rinsed his brush in the jam jar with a ringing sound and went down the short flight of stairs. He opened the door and saw a woman standing there.

'Are you the man that writes the things?' she asked. He nodded. 'I hope I'm not disturbing you.'

'No.' He felt he had to invite her in. He went up the stairs behind her and when they came to the landing she was unsure of where to go. To show her the way he went into his kitchen in front of her but realized that he should have let her go first for the sake of manners. She stood holding her basket not knowing what to do.

'Sit down,' he said and sat with his back to the table and waited.

'You do that lovely writing?' she said again. He smiled and agreed. 'I saw it in the church. That thing you did — for the people who gave money for the stained glass window.'

'The list of subscribers?'

'Do you do anything? I mean, not just religious things?'

'Yes.'

She was a woman about the same age as himself, maybe younger. Her whole appearance was tired — drab grey rain-coat, a pale oval showing just inside her knee where she had a hole in her tights, her shoes scuffed and unpolished. She looked down into her basket.

'How much would . . . ?' She seemed nervous. 'Would you do a poem?'

'Yes.'

'How much?'

'It depends on how long it is. Whether you want it framed or not. What kind of paper.'

'It's very short.' She took a woman's magazine from her basket and flicked through it looking for the page. She leafed backwards and forwards unable to find it.

'Ah, here it's.' She folded the magazine at the right page and gave it to him. 'It's only four lines.' He glanced at the page and saw the poem framed in a black box.

'I could do that very reasonable,' he said. The corners of her mouth twitched into a relieved smile. 'Five pounds.' It was obviously too much for her because the smile disappeared and she set her hand on the arm of the chair as if she was about to stand up.

'That would be framed and all,' he added.

'Maybe some time again.' She kept looking into her basket.

'On the best paper.'

'What about cheaper paper?'

'Four pounds?'

Still the woman hesitated.

'That's still a pound a line. I didn't think it would be as much as that.'

'Any less and it'd be a favour,' he said. Already he was out of pocket. He stood up to end the bargaining. Again she looked down into her raffia basket. He saw two tins of cat food at the bottom.

'All right,' she said. 'Four pounds. How soon will it be done?'

'The end of the week. Call on Friday.'

She seemed pleased and nervous that she had made a decision.

After he had shown her out he read the poem.

> The words the happy say
> Are paltry melody
> But those the silent feel
> Are beautiful —

It was by E. Dickinson. He looked at the date on the magazine and saw that it was over three years old. He closed it and set it on the shelf. It was like the woman herself, dog-eared and a bit tatty. She'd had nice eyes but her skin had been slack and almost a grey colour as if she'd been ill. Yet there had been something about her which had made him lower his price. He was not used to bargaining — most of his jobs came in the post from a small advertising agency. What they couldn't be bothered to do in Letraset they passed on to him. But the work was not regular and he couldn't rely on it — unlike the diplomas he did each year for the teacher training college.

Two days later when he wrote out the poem he was dissatisfied with it and scrapped it. For the second attempt he wrote it on one of his most expensive papers and further surprised himself by using his precious gold leaf. He hated working with the stuff, held between its protective sheets, thin as grease on tea. It curled and twitched even when he brought the heat of his fingertips near it. Yet on the finished page it looked spectacular.

On the Friday he found that, instead of working in the morning, he was tidying the flat. It was not until late evening that he heard her at the door. He turned down the volume of the radio and went to answer it. She sat down when invited and placed her hands on her lap. Her appearance had improved. She wore a mauve print summer dress, a white Arran cardigan and carried a shoulder bag, which made her seem younger. The weak sun, squared by shadows from the crossbars of the window, lit the back wall of the room behind her.

'I'm sorry,' he said, 'it's not finished.' Her mouth opened slightly in disappointment. 'I didn't know whether you wanted the name on it or not.'

'What name?'

He held out the magazine and pointed to the name beneath the poem with his bad hand. It was as if he were pointing round a corner.

'E. Dickinson.'

The woman thought for a moment then nodded. 'Put it on.' She seemed quite definite. He folded the protective paper back from his work and reached for a pen.

'Can I see it?' she asked. He handed her the written poem and watched her face.

'Aw here,' she said. 'Aw here now.' Then she spoke the poem, more to herself than to him. As she read he watched her eyes switching back and forth across the lines.

'Lovely,' she said. 'Just lovely.' He was unsure whether she was praising his work or the poem. She handed it carefully back and he turned to the table to write the name.

'Can I watch?'

'Sure thing.'

She came, almost on tiptoe, to his shoulder and watched him dip the pen and angle the spade-like nib. As he wrote, his tongue peeped out from the corner of his mouth. When he had finished he blew on the page, tilting it to the light to see if it had dried.

'Where did you learn – all this?' she asked.

'I taught myself. Just picked it up.' He stood and went over to the shelf and took down a book. 'From things like . . . this Book of Hours.'

'Ours?'

He smiled and passed it to her. She smiled too, realizing her mistake when she read the title. She opened it gingerly. The pictures were interleaved with tissue paper which slithered in the draught she made turning the pages. Each tissue bore a faint mirror image of the drawing it protected. The book was an awkward size so she sat down and laid it across her knees. She looked at the pure colours, the intricacy of the work.

'This must have taken you years,' she said.

'I didn't do it.' He smiled. 'It's a printed book.'

'Oh.' She turned another page. He stood feeling idle in front of her.

'Would you like some tea?'

She looked up and hesitated.

'It's no bother,' he said. 'I've got milk.'

'All right. That would be nice.'

He put the kettle on and set out his mug and a cup and saucer for her. The crockery rattled loudly in the silence. The kettle seemed to take ages to boil. He asked her how she had known who he was and where he lived. She said that the priest had told her after she had admired the framed list of names in the church.

When he handed her the cup and saucer she set the book carefully to one side.

'It would be just like me to spill something on it.'

He sat down opposite her. The sound of the contact between her cup and saucer made him feel nervous.

'Do you like doing this work?'

'Yes, it suits me fine. I don't have to leave the house.'

'You're like myself,' she nodded in agreement. 'Once I've the one or two bits of shopping done, I stay put. I hate the city. Always have since the day and hour I moved here. And it's getting worse. You used to be able to have a chat in Dunlop's till they changed it into a supermarket. How can you talk to the check-out girl with a queue hopping behind you?'

'You haven't lost your accent.'

'And please God I never will.'

He finished his tea and stood up. He inserted the finished poem into its frame and began to tape up the back of it. He was conscious of her watching the awkward guiding movements of his bad hand.

'It's the quiet I miss the most,' she said. 'In the country you can hear small things.'

'Would you go back?'

'Like a shot.'

'Maybe some day you will.'

She smiled at this.

With an awl he made two holes in the wood frame and began to insert the screws. He said, 'You have a cat?'

'Yes. How did you know?'

He explained about seeing the cat food in her basket.

'It thinks it's a lion,' she said. 'We have a yard at the back with pot plants and it lies flat like it's in the jungle and his tail puffs up.' He laughed at her. She went on, 'What I like about cats is the way they ignore you. There's no telling what way they feel. If I want to be popular all I have to do is rattle the tin-opener and he's all over me, purring and sharpening his back on my shins.'

'What do you call it?'

'Monroe. My husband thought that one up – not my idea at

14

all. At first we called it Marilyn until we found out it was a boy. Then we had it neutered because of the smell. We used to go a lot to the pictures.' After a pause she added, 'He's dead now God rest him.'

'Who?'

'My husband.' She set her saucer on the floor between her feet and held the cup in both hands. The sunlight on the wall behind her had changed from yellow to rose until it finally disappeared, yet the room seemed to hold on to some of the light. 'Since I got the TV there's no need to go out. All the good movies come up there.' She looked around the darkening room.

'I prefer the radio,' he said. 'It means I can work at the same time. Or look at the fire.'

He got to his feet and asked her if she felt chilly. Even though she said no, he lit the fire. The firelighter blazed in a yellow flame a few inches above the coal until it caught. It made a pleasant whirring noise.

'I couldn't be without the TV,' she said. 'It's like having another person in the house.' He smiled at her and began sweeping the hearth.

'Am I keeping you back?' she said suddenly.

'No. No. Not at all,' he said. 'It's not often anybody comes in.'

'Especially me,' she said. As the coals of the fire began to redden and burn without the help of the firelighter she talked about her childhood in the country: of making shadow pictures of monsters on the wall with a candle; of her elder sister scaring the wits out of her with stories of the devil at dances. She told of ringworm and of the woolly balaclava she had to wear to cover her bald patches; of sheep ticks and how the only way you could get them out of your skin was to burn their backsides with a hot spent match and then pluck them out while their minds were on other things. He listened to her shudder at the memory, but it was obvious from her voice that she loved it all.

When she waited for him to tell something of himself he shied away and asked her if she would like some more tea. He did tell her that he had never known his father and that his mother had died asking what time it was. Famous last words. What time is it? When he said this she held back her laughter until he laughed.

'What time *is* it?' she asked. He squinted through the gloom in the direction of the clock on the shelf and told her.

'What? I must go,' she said. But she did not get up.

'I've given you a bit of picture cord.' He hung the framed text on his finger for her to see. 'Although it's very light.'

'Light verse,' she said and laughed. He handed her his work and she held it at arm's length to admire it. He switched on the Anglepoise for her and it seemed very bright after the slow increase of dusk.

'It must be great to be an artist,' she said.

He pooh-poohed the idea saying that he couldn't draw to save his life. He said he was an artisan and added, seeing her blank look, 'A man with one skill.'

She set the picture down and opened her shoulder bag.

'Four pounds you said?' She took her purse from the bag and looked up at him, waiting for confirmation of the price.

'It doesn't matter,' he said. 'This one is free.'

'What?'

'I enjoyed doing it.'

'I wouldn't dream of it. Here,' she said and set the four pound notes on the table. He picked them up and offered them back to her. She took them and set them on the mantelpiece out of his reach.

'It's a lovely job of work. You must be paid.' She was now bustling, returning her purse to her bag, straightening her cardigan. She seemed embarrassed and he wished he had just taken the money without any fuss.

'I am very pleased with it,' she said. 'It was kind of you to offer. But no, thank you. And now I'll be off.'

He hesitated for a moment, then said, 'Let me wrap it for you.' He looked in a cupboard and found some brown paper he had saved. She sat down again to wait. He wrapped her magazine and the picture together, sellotaping down the triangular folds he had made.

A summer insect flew into the metal dome of the Anglepoise and knocked around like a tiny knuckle. She said in admiration that he was very good with his hands. He was aware of her embarrassment in the silence which followed. He held on to the parcel when he was finished and tried to think of something to say. He asked her if she had ever worked at anything. She said that for some years before she had married she had worked in a sewing-machine factory — years which had bored her stiff. He asked her if she had any children but she replied that they had not been blessed in that way. Her husband had worked with an X-ray machine before they knew the damage it could do. She averted her eyes and he did not know what to say. Eventually she stood up.

'You have more than one skill,' she said, looking at the neatness of the finished parcel. 'Thank you very much for the tea — and everything.' She stretched out to shake hands but it was an awkward clasping rather than a handshake, with his left hand in her right.

'I'll show you out,' he said, turning on the landing light. They went down the lino-covered stairs.

'Maybe I'll see you again — some time in church,' she said, looking up over her shoulder at him.

He nodded. 'Maybe. I eh . . . '

She waited for what he was going to say but he reached past her and opened the Yale lock. Sounds of children playing below echoed up the stair-well. She left smiling, clutching beneath her arm the parcel of her poem.

Upstairs again he sat down in front of the illuminated address for the bakery firm but did not begin to work. He stayed like that for a long time then punched the table hard with the knuckles of his fist so that the radio at his elbow bounced and gave a static crackle. It had been on all this time. He turned up the volume and filled the flat with the noise of voices he could not put a face to.

The Break

The cardinal sat at his large walnut desk speaking slowly and distinctly. When he came to the end of a phrase he pressed the off-switch on the microphone and thought about what to say next as he stared in front of him. On the wall above the desk was an ikon he had bought in Thessaloníki – he afterwards discovered that he had paid too much for it. It had been hanging for some months before he noticed, his attention focused by a moment of rare idleness, that Christ had a woodworm hole in the pupil of his left eye. It was inconspicuous by its position, and rather than detracting from the impact, he felt the ikon was enhanced by the authenticity of this small defect. He set the microphone on the desk, pushed his fingers up into his white hair and remained like that for some time.

'New paragraph,' he said, picking up the microphone and switching it on with his thumb. 'Christians are sometimes accused of not being people of compassion – that the Rule is more important than the good which results from it.'

The phone rang on the desk making him jump. He switched off the recorder.

'Yes?'

'Eminence, your father's just arrived. Can you see him?'

'Well, can I?'

'You're free until the Ecumenical delegation at half four.'

'I think I need a break. Will you show him up to my

sitting-room?' He made the sign of the cross and prayed, his hands joined, his index fingers pressed to his lips. At the end of his prayer he blessed himself again and stood up, stretching and flexing his aching back. He straightened his tossed hair in the mirror, flattening it with his hands, and went into the adjoining room to see if his father had managed the stairs.

The room was empty. He walked to the large bay window and looked down at the film of snow which had fallen the previous night. A black irregular track had been melted up to the front door by people coming and going but the grass of the lawns was uniformly white. The tree trunks at the far side of the garden were half black, half white where the snow had shadowed them. The wind, he noticed, had been from the north. He shuddered at the scene, felt the cold radiate from the window panes and moved back into the room to brighten up the fire. With a smile he thought it would be nice to have the old man's stout ready for him. It poured well, almost too well, with a high mushroom-coloured head. He left the bottle with some still in it, beside the glass on the mantelpiece, and stood with his back to the fire, his hands extended behind him.

When he heard a one-knuckle knock he knew it was him.

'Come in,' he called. His father pushed the door open and peered round it. Seeing the cardinal alone he smiled.

'And how's his Eminence today?'

'Daddy, it's good to see you.'

The old man joined him at the fireplace and stood in the same position. He was much smaller than his son, reaching only to his shoulder. His clothes hung on him, most obviously at the neck where his buttoned shirt and knotted tie were loose as a horse-collar. The waistband of his trousers reached almost to his chest.

The old man said, 'That north wind is cold no matter what direction it's blowing from.' The cardinal smiled. That joke was no longer funny but the old man's persistence in using it was.

'Look, I have your stout already poured for you.'

'Oh that's powerful, powerful altogether.'

The old man sat down in the armchair rubbing his hands to warm them and the cardinal passed him the stout.

'Those stairs get worse every time I climb them. Why don't you top-brass clergy live in ordinary houses?'

'It's one of the drawbacks of the job. Have you put on a little weight since the last time?'

'No, no. I'll soon not be able to sink in the bath.'

'Are you taking the stout every day?'

'Just let anyone try and stop me.'

'What about food?'

'As much as ever. But still the weight drops off. I tell you, Frank, I'll not be around for too long.'

'Nonsense. You've another ten or twenty years in you.'

The old man looked at him without smiling. There was a considerable pause.

'You know and I know that that's not true. I feel it in my bones. Sit down, son, don't loom.'

'Have you been to see the doctor again?' The cardinal sat opposite him, plucking up the front of his soutane.

'No.' The old man took a drink from his glass and wiped away the slight moustache it left with the back of his hand. 'That's in good order, that stout.'

The cardinal smiled. 'One of the advantages of the job. When I order something from the town, people tend to send me the best.'

He thought his father seemed jumpy. The old man searched for things in his pockets but brought out nothing. He fidgeted in the chair, crossing and recrossing his legs.

'How did you get in today?' asked the cardinal.

'John dropped me off. He had to get some phosphate.'

'What's it like in the hills?'

'Deeper than here, I can tell you that.'

'Did you lose any?'

'It's too soon to tell, but I don't think so. They're hardy boyos, the blackface. I've seen them carrying six inches of snow on their backs all day. It's powerful the way they keep the heat in.' The old man fidgeted in his pockets again.

'Why will you not go back to the doctor?'

The old man snorted. 'He'd probably put me off the drink as well.'

'Cigarettes are bad for you, everybody knows that. It's been proved beyond any doubt.'

'I'm off them nearly six months now and I've my nails ate to the elbow. Especially with a bottle of stout. I don't know what to do with my hands.'

'Do you not feel any better for it.'

'Damn the bit. I still cough.' The old man sipped his Guinness and topped up his glass from the remainder in the bottle. The cardinal stared over his head at the fading light of the grey sky. He could well do without this Ecumenical delegation. Of late he was not sleeping well, with the result that he tended to feel tired during the day. At meetings his eyelids were like lead and he daren't close them because if he did the quiet rise and fall of voices and the unreasonable temperature at which they kept the rooms would lull him to sleep. It had happened twice, only for seconds, when he found himself jerking awake with a kind of snort and looking around to see if anyone had noticed. This afternoon he would much prefer to take to his bed and that was not like him. He should go and see a doctor himself, even though he knew no one could prescribe for weariness. He looked at his father's yellowed face. Several times the old man opened his mouth to speak but said nothing. He was sitting with his fingers threaded through each other, the backs of his hands resting on his thighs. The cardinal was aware that it was exactly how he himself sometimes sat. People said they were the spit of each other. He remembered as a small child the clenched hands of his father as he played a game with him. 'Here is the church, here is the steeple.' The thumbs parted, the hands turned over and the interlaced fingers waggled up at him. 'Open the doors and here are the people.' Now his father's hands lay as if the game was finished but they had not the energy to separate from each other. At last the old man broke the silence.

'I'm trying to put everything in order at home. You know – for the big day.' He smiled. 'I was going through all the papers and stuff I'd gathered over the years.' He pulled out a pair of glasses from his top pocket with pale flesh-coloured frames. The cardinal knew they were his mother's, plundered from her bits and pieces after she died.

'Why don't you get yourself a proper pair of glasses?'

'My sight is perfectly good – it's just that there's not much of it. I found this.' His father fumbled into his inside pocket and pulled out two sheets of paper. He hooked the legs of the spectacles behind his ears, briefly inspected the sheets and handed one to his son.

'Do you remember that?'

The cardinal saw his own neat handwriting from some thirty years ago. The letter was addressed to his mother and father from Rome. It was an ordinary enough letter which tried to describe his new study-bedroom – the dark-brightness of the room in the midday sun when the green shutters were closed. The letter turned to nostalgia and expressed a longing to be back on the farm in the hills. The cardinal looked up at his father.

'I don't recall writing this. I remember the room but not the letter.' His father stretched and handed him the second sheet.

'It was in the same envelope as this one.'

The cardinal unfolded the page from its creases.

Dear Daddy,

Don't read this letter out. It is for you alone. I enclose another 'ordinary letter' for you to show Mammy because she will expect to see what I have said.

I write to you because I want you to break it gradually to her that I am not for the priesthood. It would be awful for her if I just arrived through the door and said that I wasn't up to it. But that's the truth of it.

These past two months I have prayed my knees numb asking for guidance. I have black rings under my eyes from lack of sleep. To have gone so far – five years of study and prayer – and still to be unsure. I believe now that I can serve God in a better way, a different way from the priesthood.

I know how much it means to her. Please be gentle in preparing her.

'Yes, I remember this one.'

'I thought you might like to have it.'

'Yes thank you, I would.' The cardinal let the letter fall back into its original folds and set it on the occasional table beside him.

'And did you prepare her?'

'Yes. Until I got your next letter.'

'What did she say?'

22

'She thought it was just me — doubting Thomas she called me.'

'It was a bad time. Every time I smell garlic I remember it.' He knelt to poke the fire. 'Another bottle of stout?'

'It's so good I won't refuse you.' His father finished what was left in the glass. The cardinal poured a new one and set it by the chair. The old man stared vacantly at the far wall and the cardinal looked out of the bay window. The sky was dark and heavy with snow. It was just starting to fall again, large flakes floating down and curving up when they came near to the glass.

'You'd better not leave it too late going home,' he said. The old man opened his mouth to speak but stopped.

'What's wrong?'

'Nothing.' His father knuckled his left eye. 'Except . . . '

'Except what?'

'I suppose I showed that letter to you . . . for a purpose.'

'As if I didn't know.'

'I want to make a confession.' Seeing his son raise an eyebrow the old man smiled. 'Not that kind of confession. A real one. And it's very hard to say it.' The cardinal sat down.

'Well?'

The old man smiled a smile that stopped in the middle. Then he put his head back to rest it on the white linen chair-back.

'I've lost the faith,' he said. The cardinal was silent. The snow kept up an irregular ticking at the window pane. 'I don't believe that there is a God.'

'Sorry I'm not with you. Is it that . . . ?'

'Don't stop me. I've gone over this in my head for months now.' The cardinal nodded silently. 'I want to say it once and for all — and only to you. I have not believed for twenty-five years. But what could I do? A son who was looked up to by everyone around him — climbing through the ranks of the Church like nobody's business — the youngest-ever cardinal. How could I stop going to Mass, to the sacraments? How could I? I never told your mother because it would have killed her long before her time.'

'God rest her.'

'Frank, there is no God. Religion is a marvellous institution, full of great, good people – but it's founded on a lie. Not a deliberate lie – a mistake.'

'You're wrong. I *know* that God exists. Apart from what I feel in here,' the cardinal pointed to his chest, 'there are convincing proofs.'

'Proofs are no good for God. That's Euclid.' The old man was no longer looking at his son but staring obliquely down at the fire. 'I know in my bones that I'll not be around too long, Frank. I had to tell somebody because I would be a hypocrite if I took it to the grave with me. I am telling you because we're . . . because I . . . admire you.' The cardinal shook his head and looked down at his knees.

'Do you know what the amazing thing is?' said his father. 'I don't miss Him. You'd think that somebody who'd been reared like me would be lost. You know – the way they taught you to talk to Jesus as a friend – the way you felt you were being looked after – the way you were told it was the be-all and the end-all, and for that suddenly to stop and me not even miss it. That was a shock. I'll tell you this, Frank, when your mother died I missed her a thousand times more.'

'Yes, I'm sure you did.'

'To tell the God's honest truth I miss the cigarettes more.'

The cardinal smiled weakly. 'If this was a public debate . . . ' He seemed to sag in his chair. His shoulders went down and his hands lay in his lap, palm upwards. The snow was getting heavier and finer and was hissing at the window. The old man looked over his shoulder at the fading light.

'I'd better think of going. I wonder where John's got to?'

'Did he say he'd pick you up here?'

'Yes.' The old man looked his son straight in the eye. 'I'm sorry,' he said, 'but I wanted to be honest with you because . . . ' he looked into his empty glass, 'because I . . . '

'You can stay the night and we can talk.'

'There's not much more to be said.' The old man got up and stood at the window looking down. He looked so frail that his son imagined he could see through him. He remembered him at the celebration after his ordination in a hotel in Rome banging the table with a soup-spoon for order and then making a speech about having two sons, one who looked after the body's needs and the other who looked after the soul's. When he had finished, as always at functions, he sang 'She Moved thro' the Fair'. The old man looked at his watch.

'Where is he?' He put his hands in his jacket pockets, leaving his thumbs outside, and paced the alcove of the bay window.

'If I may stand Pascal's Wager on its head,' said the cardinal, 'if you do not believe and are as genuinely good a man as you are, then God will accept you. You will have won through even though you bet wrongly.'

The old man shrugged his shoulders without turning. 'The way I feel that's neither here nor there. But this talk has done me good. I hope it hasn't hurt you too much.'

'It must have been a great burden for you. Now you have just given it to me.' Seeing the concern in his father's face he added, 'But at least I have God to help me bear it. I will pray for you always.'

'It's not as black as I paint it. Over the years there was a kind of contentment. I had lost one thing but gained another. It concentrates the mind wonderfully knowing that this is all we can expect. A glass of stout tastes even better.' The old man took one hand out of his pocket and shaded his eyes, peering out into the snow. 'Ah there he is now. It must be bad, he has the headlights on.'

'Does John know all this?'

'No. You are the only one. But please don't worry. I'll continue as I've done up till now. I'll go to mass, receive the sacraments. It's hard to teach an old dog new tricks.'

'That's the farthest thing from my mind.'

The old man turned and came across the room. The cardinal still sat, his hands open. His father took him by the right hand and leaned down and kissed him with his lips on the cheekbone. The hand was light and dry as polystyrene, the lips like paper.

The cardinal had not cried since the death of his mother and even then he had waited until he was alone but now he could not stop the tears rising.

'I will see you again soon,' said his father. Then, noticing his son's brimming eyes, he said, 'Frank, if I'd known that I wouldn't have told you.'

'It's not because of that,' said the cardinal. 'Not that at all.'

After he had seen his father to the door and had a few words with his brother — mostly about the need for them to get home quickly before the roads became impassable — the cardinal went back to his office. He sat for a long time with his elbows on the desk and his head in his hands. He blessed himself slowly as if his right arm was weighted and said his prayer-before-work. He picked up the microphone and spoke.

'The Church has a public and a private face. The Church of Authority and the Church of Compassion, the Church of Rules and the Church of Forgiveness. What the public face lacks is empathy. This was not so with Jesus. We who are within the Church must strive to narrow the gap that exists between . . . them. We know that . . . ' His voice trailed away and he switched off the microphone. Then, with an effort that made him groan, he slid from the chair to kneel on the floor. The cushioned Rexine of the chair-seat hissed slowly back to its original shape. He joined his hands in prayer so that the knuckles formed a platform for his chin. When the words would not come he lowered his hands, and his interlocked fingers were ready to waggle up at him as in the childish game. He parted his hands and laid them flat on the chair.

In the car with John the old man sat forward in his seat watching the brightness of the snow slanting in the headlights.

'Did you do what you had to do?' he asked.

'Aye — it's all in the back,' said John. 'What do I smell?'

'Stout.'

'The odour of sanctity.'

The windscreen wipers, on intermittent, purred and slapped. In front of them the road was white except for two yellow-dark ruts.

'That snow's thick.'

'It'll get worse as we climb,' said John.

'Just follow the tracks of the boyo that's gone before and we'll be all right.'

From then on there was silence as John drove slowly and with great care up into the mountains.

The Drapery Man

I rise every day and walk the half mile up the hill to Jordan's place with his dog at my heels. I have to take it slowly, for the sake of the dog. It is a small brown and white short-haired terrier which he christened Pangur-Ban. Each evening I take her home with me to prevent Jordan, as he says, 'taking the air on the patio and tramping in shite, then walking it throughout the house.' She waddles and her tongue hangs out. Her paws slip on the stone mosaic footpath. The dog is as old in dog years as Jordan.

Today he has asked me to bring tennis balls. I have bought half a dozen packed like eggs in a plastic container which crackles as I walk up the hill.

I used to live with Jordan until things became intolerable. Then he rented a place for me, small but with a good view over the Atlantic. I am on my own when I want to be, which suits me. It suits him as well because a blind man needs to live on his own. He can remember where the furniture is, where he last set something down. The only drawback, Jordan tells me, is that he will probably die on his own, and that frightens him. He is in his seventies, has a bad heart and is expecting the worst.

He is sitting in a director's canvas chair in the middle of the converted barn tilting his head back to the light waiting for me. As soon as he hears the door he shouts, 'Here, girl.' Pangur-Ban barks twice and runs to him. Even if she doesn't bark he can hear her pads and claws on the stone floor. She wags her tail so much that her whole body seems to move. He scratches her head.

'And my drapery man.' I kiss him like we were father and son and lift the dog up on his knee. He caresses the back of my thigh.

He laughs, 'This morning when I awoke I had a little stiffness in my joints. One in particular.' He laughs. 'Isn't that good at my age?'

'I bet it didn't last long,' I say, moving away from him.

He is on edge — he wants to start a new painting even though we haven't finished the previous three. I have spent the last few days making canvases to his specifications — one seven feet by fourteen and then a smaller one, six by three.

'Give the big one a wash of turps and burnt sienna — as dilute as possible.'

Before he went blind completely he would inspect my colour mixing. He would tell me equal parts viridian and cobalt with just a smear of black and I would mix it for him. He then would bend over the tray, like a jeweller, squinting with his one good eye at the colour. 'Yes it's right,' or, 'More black.' It was about this time that he began to wear the glasses with the mudguards at the sides.

Since he has totally lost his sight he uses other things to denote colour. 'The blue vase beside the window — the shadowed side of it,' or, 'The maroon cover of *Marius the Epicurean*.' I begin to search the bookshelves.

'Who's it by?'

'Pater.' He gives a little sigh. 'Walter Pater — an English fuckin hooligan, if ever there was one.'

I find it and hold it up to the light. Jordan says, 'As a book it's rubbish — but it's the right colour.'

Occasionally he uses previous pictures of his own as a reference.

'I want the umber to be exactly what I used in "Harbinger Three".' And I have to try and remember! Reproductions are only the merest approximation. Colour slides are better but still their colour values are not accurate. Sometimes, when he is being particularly difficult or pernickety, I have to admit to cheating. I will tell him I remember the colour and have got it exactly. He has no way of knowing.

I change into what was a navy blue boiler suit. It is japped and stippled with every colour he has made me use. Because of the heat the only other thing I wear is my underpants. In the old days this used to drive him wild. I squeeze a fat worm of burnt sienna into a roller tray and drown it in turps.

He uses masking tape a lot. That way he can feel with his fingers what he can see in his mind.

'Three verticals of white, the three-quarter inch, spaced like cricket stumps.' I peel off the tape when the paint has dried, leaving livid white.

Sometimes he will say, 'Let me make a shape,' and approach the canvas with a stick of charcoal. He will draw big and simple out of the darkness of his head.

He has an amazing visual memory. To divide up his canvases he will refer me to a book of Flags of the World.

'The three bands should be like the South Vietnamese flag stood on its end,' or, 'The band at the bottom should be as broad as the blue stripe in the Israeli flag.'

The work is as hard as painting a room. He sits listening to the click of the roller and my breathing, fondling the bones of the dog's head. Sometimes her upright ears flick like a cat's when touched.

When the canvas is covered I sit down for a break but he becomes impatient with me.

'Get out what we did yesterday,' he says. I turn the outermost canvas from the wall to face him. He drops the dog on the floor and comes over to me, his arms out in front of him. His hands touch the surface and skim lightly over it feeling the layers of paint with the tips of his fingers, the direction of the brush strokes.

'That's the magenta?'

'Yes.'

'It's too loosely brushed. I wish you'd sprayed it.'

'Why didn't you say?'

'Could you bear to do it again?'

'I suppose so. Jordan, you're a perfectionist.'

'Oh fuck.' He cups one hand over his eyes. 'This is like trying to thread a needle with gloves on.'

I begin squeezing out some magenta.

'Why do you go on doing this?'

'Somebody's got to pay the rent − the rents. Two places.'

'Jordan − come on. You get the price of a house for one of these things.'

'Things! You philistine gobshite.'

'I didn't mean it that way.'

'It's the way it came out − it was your tone. A middle-class English whine.'

'The Irish are racists,' I say and storm out of the barn.

He shouts after me, 'It wasn't us who fucked up half the world.'

It takes me until midday to calm down.

'Jordan! Lunch!' He comes out on to the shaded side of the patio to join me. It is easy to prepare. A bottle of chilled Verde, some bread and pâté. He likes the local pâté and I spread each circle of crusty bread with a thick roof of the stuff. Three small pieces on a plate, easily located, easily eaten. The bread crackles as he bites into it.

'Oh for a piece of bread that doesn't bleed your gums,' he says, chewing. 'Right now I'd pay a fiver for a slice of Pan loaf. Something soft that'll stick to the roof of your mouth.'

I don't answer him and there is a long silence. He feels this for a while, then says, 'With regard to this morning. I still have pictures in my head which have to come out but they are limited by the clumsy technique I have to use. Imagine having to paint − not with a brush − but with an English gobshite.' This time it sounds funny and he senses my reaction. 'In the 'fifties I was attracted to Hard Edge. Now it is all that is left to me. I see the way Beethoven heard. For that reason alone we must continue.'

I am his eyes and his right hand. He will occasionally ask me to describe things. If it becomes a chore he will know from the tone of my voice and stop me.

'The Atlantic today is Mediterranean blue.' He laughs obediently. 'And at this moment I can see two yachts, one a mere arrowhead with a white sail, the other much closer, running behind a blue and white spinnaker.' That kind of thing.

He will always have a cutting remark to end with, like, 'It pays to increase your word power.'

I also read to him. He has become blind so late in life that he is unwilling to learn the new skill of Braille. He likes Beckett – even laughs at him – but I find his prose almost impossible to read aloud and quite, quite meaningless. I come from the kind of house where if my father saw me with a book in my hand he'd say, 'Can you not find something better to do?'

Flann O'Brien is also a favourite – especially the pieces from the *Irish Times* – but my English accent is intrusive and my attempts at an Irish one, so Jordan tells me, disastrous. He appreciates my version of a Home Counties voice reading the test match reports which arrive a day late from England. But because they are always a day late his excitement and anticipation is still the same.

'One of my great regrets is that I'll never see this fella Botham play.' This from a man who hasn't left Portugal for twenty-five years.

In the winter when cricket reports are scarce occasionally he asks me to read to him from Wisden's Cricketers' Almanack.

'A lizard has just appeared on the wall of your bedroom and is soaking up the sun. Its spine is an S. Why do they never end up straight?'

'We're all bent,' says Jordan and gropes for his wine glass. He drains what's left and stands. I lead him back to the barn and he lies down on the divan for a nap. He claims that he can sleep better during the day than at night. I go into the house to wash up the dishes, tidy and make his bed.

I first met him while on holiday in the Algarve about twenty years ago. My mother had been recently widowed and dreaded the thought of spending Christmas in the house. She also dreaded being alone and asked me to accompany her. At the time I was a student of Engineering Drawing and the holidays were sufficiently long to allow me to do this without missing anything. Mother and I had been there about a fortnight and were becoming bored with each other. Both of us admitted to a longing to hear English spoken again. We met Jordan coming out of a bistro. Because he was drunk he was speaking in English, shouting it over his shoulder at those who had annoyed him. Despite the fact that his accent was Irish and that he was well on in drink Mother pounced on him, so avid was she for conversation with someone other than me. She brought him back to our hotel for coffee.

Jordan Fitzgerald was his name. He was then a splendid-looking man in his early fifties, lean and tanned with a beard which was whitening in streaks. Mother simpered before him and asked him what he did.

'I'm a cricketer who paints.'

She became, if it was possible, more obsequious when she discovered just how famous an artist he was. She knew nothing of painting — for her, degrees of realism were degrees of excellence and all our house in London could boast of was a number of Victorian prints my father had looted from his own mother's house. Another factor which impressed her was the price his pictures could command. When she eventually got to see some of his work her comment to me afterwards was, 'I wouldn't give you tuppence for it.'

'Mother, he is one of Ireland's greatest artists and has the accolade of having work in the Tate.'

'I don't care where he's worked. I wouldn't hang one of those things on my wall. If your father was alive he could tell him what he was doing wrong.'

She thought his interest was in her, handsome in her mid-forties, but I knew by his eyes that I was the focus of his attention.

On the second last night of our holiday we had all been drinking heavily in our hotel and Mother went off to powder her nose.

Jordan leaned forward and said to me in a voice that was hushed and serious, 'You are beautiful. Why don't you walk up the hill later?'

I nodded and cautioned him with a look, seeing Mother coming back. He added, 'And I'll show you my retchings.' We both laughed uncontrollably at this.

'Have I missed a joke?' said Mother.

'I was just telling your handsome boy a story which would offend the ears of a lovely English lady like yourself. I hope you'll forgive me.'

She smiled coyly — a smile which said they are just men together.

But I did go to his house later that night. We had sex twice and I stayed with him the next night as well — or at least slipped back into the hotel at five in the morning. Mother remarked on how tired I looked and I proved it by sleeping on the train until Paris.

In the spring Jordan wrote to me one of the shortest letters I have ever received inviting me in almost gruff terms to spend the summer with him. In a PS he said that Mother would also be welcome — in September. I had just finished my course with the highest commendation and felt I deserved the summer off before looking for work. Mother agreed both to my going and to her visit later.

Once I asked him why he had left Ireland.

'It's no place for a homosexual painter who doesn't believe in God,' he said, then added after a moment's thought, 'Indeed it's no place for a heterosexual painter who's a Catholic.' But he cherished aspects of his country. He claimed to be able to quote the label on any bottle of Irish whiskey word for word. I tested him when I arrived back from London after Mother's funeral. I had brought him a bottle of Bushmills and challenged him to make good his boast.

'The label is black like a church window, with a gold rim. It has a vermilion band like a cummerbund across its middle and beneath that is a scatter of gold coins.'

'Correct. And the words. You have to quote the words before you can sample it.' He held his head in his hands and screwed up his eyes, smiling.

'Special old Irish whiskey. Black Bush. Original grant to distil — sixteen-', he paused slapping the top of his head, 'oh-eight. Blended and bottled by the inverted commas Old Bushmills, close inverted commas, Distillery Company Limited, Bushmills, County Antrim. Product of Ireland.'

'Correct — you're a genius.'

'There's more. At the bottom it says "registered label".'

He stood and we kissed. He told me how he'd missed me and asked with concern about Mother's cremation.

The nearest I could come to that party trick was to recite the French side of the HP Sauce bottle. '*Cette Sauce de haute qualité* . . . etc.' Jordan made me do it for his friends.

Afterwards he would always announce, 'He passed his exams with the highest condemnation.'

Sometimes I lie awake at night wondering what I will do when Jordan dies. I have given up my career and my life for him. I remember once reading about Eric Fenby, Delius's amanuensis, and feeling sorry for him. An intelligent man in touch with such talent but devoid of actual genius himself. I have become involved in painting but am useless at it — as useless as Beckett's secretary is at writing, if he has one — as useless as Beckett is, come to think of it.

It has occurred to me that I could, with the right amount of secrecy, continue to produce Jordan Fitzgeralds for a number of years to come, and say to the dealer that they came from stock. But that would necessitate getting him to sign blank canvases. I have never plucked up enough courage to ask him to do such a thing.

I think that Jordan took me on because I would do what I was told — to the letter — exactly. Engineering Drawing is that kind of science. Even then Jordan must have had intimations of his coming blindness. He said a philistine was what he wanted. If I was artistic it would interfere with the translation of his vision on to canvas.

After I had finished my first painting under his direction he went up to it and looked all over its surface from six inches. He nodded with approval.

'I'll call you my drapery man.'

'What?'

'An eighteenth-century caper. Portrait painters got a man in to do the time-consuming bits — the lace and the satin stuff. The best of them was Vanaken. Hogarth drew this man's funeral with all the best painters in London behind the coffin weeping and gnashing their teeth.'

The sound of the Hoover, even from the distance of the house, wakens him because when I switch it off I hear him calling me. I go across to the barn.

'Are we ready to start again?' he says.

'Okay.'

'If you have fully recovered from your high dudgeon.'

'I have.'

He puts on a querulous voice and says, 'Question. What particular altitude is dudgeon inevitably? Answer. High.' He laughs and slaps his knees.

'Did you take your pills?' He shakes his head and I have to go all the way back to the house and bring them to him.

When he has swallowed them he says, 'I want you to scumble the bottom third with sap green.'

'In a straight line?'

'No, tilt it slightly – like the top side of a T-square.'

When Mother came down that September I was still living with Jordan, but she thought nothing of it. I had my own room. He had his. Mother always thought sex was something which happened in a bedroom at night when everyone else had retired. I had warned Jordan to be discreet and he only approached me during the early evening when she went for her walk to the cliff top to feel the cool breeze come off the sea.

'It's my favourite time of day,' she said.

'Then why do you come here? In England it is that temperature all the time – and even cooler.' I was annoyed with her because she had made no mention of going home and it was the first of October. When I finally did broach the subject she said that she was waiting for me to go home with her.

'I am staying here.'

'But how will you live? You have to get a job.'

'Jordan is now my employer.'

'And what do you do, might I ask?'

'I help him. Make up canvases. Clean his brushes. Keep the place in order. Do the shopping. Allow him time to concentrate on painting.'

'A houseboy.'

'If you like. In pleasant surroundings at a temperature I enjoy. With one of the great artists of the twentieth century.'

Before I met Jordan I knew nothing of painting. But he got me interested – gave me books to read, pictures to look at. He would deride his renowned contemporaries – 'Patrick's a total wanker', 'McGill's line has all the subtlety of a car skid.'

All this bewildered me at the time, because I thought them

all equally poor. I was more convinced of the worth of the Post-Impressionists. Jordan thought Picasso good enough to envy, and Bonnard. He thought Matisse uneven and as for Manet – he was a disgrace.

When I have finished scumbling with the sap green Jordan says, 'Make up a bowl of black and one of turquoise – straight from the tube. A third turps.' He takes the container of tennis balls and cracks it open. His fingers hesitate on their furry yellow surface. He removes one and lays his index finger diagonally across it. 'Watch the spin,' he says and flicks the ball across the barn. It bounces once, breaking back on itself about six inches. Pangur-Ban lurches forward as if to chase it, then decides not to and wags her tail.

'My brother and I used to play cricket, at a time when it was neither profitable nor popular. We had a backyard at home about ten by twelve and we had stumps chalked on one wall. The fielders were buckets – they could catch you out if the ball went in without bouncing. But there were always arguments about when the stumps were hit. We bowled underarm with a tennis ball and solved the arguments by soaking it. Then it left a wet mark on the stumps which could not be denied.'

Once a year a furniture van, hired by Jordan's London dealer, arrives and the driver and myself load the paintings on to it. For the last five years it has been the same man. He has no interest in art whatsoever: 'They're big this year,' he says, or, 'He's using a lot of green.'

'He's Irish,' I say.

'Careful. Easy. He'll go mad if you scrape one of these things.' The van-driver speaks to me in whispers, which I find insulting. Somehow his conspiracy makes me no more than a houseboy. I resent this but do not know how to reprimand him. It's not worth it for once a year.

Jordan rarely, if ever, goes out.

'There's no point,' he says. 'One darkness is the same as another. The only way you can change the landscape for me is to bring in flowers – or pine cones – or fart, for that matter.'

The only place he goes is the bank in Albufeira. Once every three months I phone a taxi and take him there. I lead him into the bank by the arm and the manager is waiting to take his other arm.

'*Bom dia*, Jordan.' They go into an office while I wait at the counter. He has *never* told me how much he is worth – I suppose he has no idea himself.

When I have made up the bowls of colour he asks me to float a tennis ball in each.

'You would be as well to wear rubber gloves,' he says. 'Now I want you to press the black ball on that mimosa area to the left of the three masking strips – about an inch out. The outline should be fuzzy. Then I want a pyramid of them – just like the medals on the Black Bush bottle.'

We ceased to be lovers many years ago but I still feel a sense of responsibility to him. I can't leave him, particularly now that he is blind. Nobody else would put up with him. I find my release and relaxation elsewhere. The beaches here teem with beautiful bodies – the roads are full of young bare-chested boys who drive about on motorbikes which sound like hornets. But it is becoming more difficult year by year. I am forty-three and beginning to thicken. I have breasts like a teenage girl. I'm sure Jordan knows of my affairs but I have never told him.

My annoyance with him reaches peaks and I have walked out on him many times. One of the worst was when I asked him – point-blank – if he had screwed my mother and he said in his own defence, 'Not often.'

After that I slept on the beach for a week. When I went back he was very kind to me – told me that artists were a race apart. They did things differently because of the albatross of their sensitivity. I think on this occasion he even apologized to me.

The normal and frequent rows we have end with him yelling at me, 'Go, go. And good riddance! I am as weak as any other man.' But I always come back. It is not for the money that I am staying on – if I know Jordan he will leave me a year's wages and the rest will go to a Cricketing Trust, or Pangur-Ban.

When I have finished dabbing the tennis balls on the surface of the canvas he asks, 'How does it look?'

'Fine. Actually it looks really good.'

'Ectually,' he spits the word out. 'I wouldn't have told you to do it if I hadn't *known* it would look good.'

'The rubber S shows up negatively in some of them.'

'I knew it would.'

I lead him to the canvas and kneel him down in front of it.

'I cannot see it but I'm sure it has all the sadness of a thing finished.' He feels for the right-angled sides of the corner then signs it with a charcoal stick in his highstepping signature.

He stands with an effort and says, 'I'd like you to do my beard.' He stretches and sits again in his canvas chair. I lift the sharpest scissors and begin to cut his beard close. He likes it to look like a week's growth.

'Pure white,' I say.

'What past tense as applied to the propulsion of motor vehicles is snow as white as?'

I think for a while then guess. 'Driven.'

He caresses my buttocks and says, 'You're coming on.'

'Don't do that or I'll cut your lip.' He takes his hand away from me.

'Wait,' says Jordan. 'Get a saucer. Keep the hairs for me.'

'What?'

'Let's keep the hairs — they're white. Save them and use them in a painting some time.'

'Are you serious, Jordan?'

'Yes I am.'

I go and wash a saucer and dry it, then continue clipping his beard on to it.

'I never know with you, whether you're sending me up or not.'

'It's a great idea. Hairy paintings. I've used sand in the past — but to . . . I'd like to put something of myself into just one of these images.'

'You *are* joking.'

'If I could find the right medium to float them in. Save them anyway — let me think about it.'

I put the clippings from the saucer into a polythene bag, tie the neck in a knot and put it on the shelf.

'I want you to read to me tonight. Also I want to get drunk.'

I know that this is a command for me to stay with him until whatever hour he chooses and put him safely into his bed. His capacity for drink is prodigious and his aggression proportional to the amount taken. The only thing in my favour is that he is now physically weak and I can master him. He used to throw things at me but that ceased when he finally became blind.

'Very well,' I say. It has the makings of a long and difficult night.

The last session — about three weeks ago — he said to me, 'I'm getting through it quite well.'

'What?'

'My life. There can't be long to go now. The thought of suicide is a great consolation. It has helped me through manys a bad night. Do you know who said that?'

'No.'

'I didn't think you would. You have a Reader's Digest grasp of the world. Just promise me one thing — don't slot me into one of those wall cupboards in the graveyard.'

'But I will. And I'll put one of those nice ceramic photos of you on the door with little roses all round it.'

'Burn me and fritter my ashes on the ocean.'

Inevitably halfway down the bottle he will begin to cry. The tears will fill his eyes and spill over on to his cheeks and wet his beard. When he stops and blows his nose thoroughly in that navy hanky of his, he will say, 'It's amazing that the eyes work so well in that function but in no other way.'

If he cries tonight I'll really put the knife in — get even with him for today's nastiness. I'll ask him if he wants his tears kept. If he wants a phial of them put in one of his paintings. If I do say this there will be a God-awful row. He'll wreck the place. The one thing he cannot stand is to have his work ridiculed — even by me.

But no matter how furious the fight, the bitching, the name-calling, I will be back in the morning with Pangur-Ban at my heels. There is now a kind of unspoken acceptance that I am here until he dies.

More than just the Disease

As he unpacked his case Neil kept hearing his mother's voice. *Be tidy at all times, then no one can surprise you.* This was a strange house he'd come to, set in the middle of a steep terraced garden. Everything in it seemed of an unusual design; the wardrobe in which he hung his good jacket was of black lacquer with a yellow inlay of exotic birds. *A little too ornate for my taste − vulgar almost.* And pictures − there were pictures hanging everywhere, portraits, landscapes, sketches. *Dust gatherers.* The last things in his case were some comics and he laid them with his ironed and folded pyjamas on the pillow of the bottom bunk and went to join the others.

They were all sitting in the growing dark of the large front room, Michael drinking hot chocolate, Anne his sister with her legs flopped over the arm of the chair, Dr Middleton squeaking slowly back and forth in the rocking-chair while his wife moved around preparing to go out.

'Now, boys, you must be in bed by ten thirty at the latest. Anne can sit up until we come back if she wants. We'll not be far away and if anything does happen you can phone "The Seaview".' She spent some time looking in an ornamental jug for a pen to write down the number. 'I can find nothing in this house yet.'

'We don't need Anne to babysit,' said Michael. 'We're perfectly capable of looking after ourselves. Isn't that right Neil?' Neil nodded. He didn't like Michael involving him in an argument with the rest of the family. He had to have the tact of a guest; sit on the fence yet remain Michael's friend.

'Can we not stay up as late as Anne?' asked Michael.

'Anne is fifteen years of age. Please, Michael, it's been a long day. Off to bed.'

'But Mama, Neil and I . . .'

'Michael.' The voice came from the darkness of the rocking-chair and had enough threat in it to stop Michael. The two boys got up and went to their bedroom.

Neil lifted his pyjamas and went to the bathroom. He dressed for bed buttoning the jacket right up to his neck and went back with his clothes draped over his arm. Michael was half-dressed.

'That was quick,' he said. He bent his thin arms, flexing his biceps. 'I only wear pyjama bottoms. Steve McQueen, he-man,' and he thumped his chest before climbing to the top bunk. They lay and talked and talked — about their first year at the school, how lucky they had been to have been put in the same form, who they hated most. The Crow with his black gown and beaky nose, the Moon with his pallid round face, wee Hamish with his almost mad preoccupation with ruling red lines. Once Neil had awkwardly ruled a line which showed the two bumps of his fingers protruding beyond the ruler and wee Hamish had pounced on it.

'What are these bumps? Is this a drawing of a camel, boy?' Everybody except Neil had laughed and if there was one thing he couldn't abide it was to be laughed at. A voice whispered that it was a drawing of his girlfriend's chest.

Neil talked about the Scholarship examination and the day he got his results. When he saw the fat envelope on the mat he knew his life would change — if you got the thin envelope you had failed, a fat one with coloured forms meant that you had passed. What Neil did not say was that his mother had cried, kneeling in the hallway hugging and kissing him. He had never seen anyone cry with happiness before and it worried him a bit. Nor did he repeat what she had said with her eyes shining. *Now you'll be at school with the sons of doctors and lawyers.*

Anne opened the door and hissed into the dark.

'You've got to stop talking right now. Get to sleep.' She was in a cotton nightdress which became almost transparent with the light of the hallway behind her. Neil saw her curved shape outlined to its margins. He wanted her to stay there but she slammed the door.

After that they whispered and had a farting competition. They heard Michael's father and mother come in, make tea and go to bed. It was ages before either of them slept. All the time Neil was in agonies with his itch but he did not want to scratch in case Michael should feel the shaking communicated to the top bunk.

In the morning Neil was first awake and tiptoed to the bathroom with all his clothes to get dressed. He took off his pyjama jacket and looked at himself in the mirror. Every morning he hoped that it would have miraculously disappeared overnight but it was still there crawling all over his chest and shoulders: his psoriasis — a redness with an edge as irregular as a map and the skin flaking and scumming off the top. Its pattern changed from week to week but only once had it appeared above his collar line. That week his mother had kept him off school. He turned his back on the mirror and put on a shirt, buttoning it up to the neck. He wondered if he should wear a tie to breakfast but his mother's voice had nothing to say on the subject.

Breakfast wasn't a meal like in his own house when he and his mother sat down at table and had cereal and tea and toast with sometimes a boiled egg. Here people just arrived and poured themselves cornflakes and went off to various parts of the room, or even the house, to eat them. The only still figure was the doctor himself. He sat at the corner of the table reading the *Scotsman* and drinking coffee. He wore blue running shoes and no socks and had a T-shirt on. Except for his receding M-shaped hairline he did not look at all like a doctor. In Edinburgh anytime Neil had seen him he wore a dark suit and a spotted bow-tie.

Anne came in. '*Guten Morgen, mein Papa*. Hello Neil.' She was bright and washed with her yellow hair in a knot on the top of her head. Neil thought she was the most beautiful girl he had ever seen up close. She wore a pair of denims cut down to shorts so that there were frayed fringes about her thighs. She also had what his mother called *a figure*. She ate her cornflakes noisily and the doctor did not even raise his eyes from the paper. *Close your mouth when you're eating, please. Others have to live with you.*

'Some performance last night, eh Neil?' she said.

'Pardon?'

'Daddy, they talked till all hours.'

Her father turned a page of the paper and his hand groped out like a blind man's to find his coffee.

'Sorry,' said Neil.

'I'm only joking,' said Anne and smiled at him. He blushed because she looked directly into his eyes and smiled at him as if she liked him. He stumbled to his feet.

'Thank you for the breakfast,' he said to the room in general and went outside to the garden where Michael was sitting on the steps.

'Where did you get to? You didn't even excuse yourself from the table,' said Neil.

'I wasn't at the table, small Fry,' said Michael. He was throwing pea-sized stones into an ornamental pond at a lower level.

'One minute you were there and the next you were gone.'

'I thought it was going to get heavy.'

'What?'

'I know the signs. The way the old man reads the paper. Coming in late last night.'

'Oh.'

Neil lifted a handful of multi-coloured gravel and fed the pieces singly into his other hand and lobbed them at the pool. They made a nice plip noise.

'Watch it,' said Michael. He stilled Neil's throwing arm with his hand. 'Here comes Mrs Wan.'

'Who's she?'

An old woman in a bottle-green cardigan and baggy mouse-coloured trousers came stepping one step at a time down towards them. She wore a puce-coloured hat like a turban and, although it was high summer, a pair of men's leather gloves.

'Good morning, boys,' she said. Her voice was the most superior thing Neil had ever heard, even more so than his elocution teacher's. 'And how are you this year, Benjamin?'

'Fine. This is my friend Neil Fry.' Neil stood up and nodded. She was holding secateurs and a flat wooden basket. He knew

43

that she would find it awkward to shake hands so he did not offer his.

'How do you do? What do you think of my garden, young man?'

'It's very good. Tidy.'

'Let's hope it remains that way throughout your stay,' she said and continued her sideways stepping down until she reached the compost heap at the bottom beyond the ornamental pool.

'Who is she?' asked Neil.

'She owns the house. Lets it to us for the whole of the summer.'

'But where does she live when you're here?'

'Up the back in a caravan. She's got ninety million cats.' Mrs Wan's puce turban threaded in and out of the flowers as she weeded and pruned. It was a dull overcast day and the wind was moving the brightly-coloured rose blooms.

'Fancy a swim?' asked Michael.

'Too cold. Anyway I told you I can't swim.'

'You don't have to swim. Just horse around. It's great.'

'Naw.'

Michael threw his whole handful of gravel chirping into the pond and went up the steps to the house.

That afternoon the shelf of cloud moved inland and the sky over the Atlantic became blue. The wind dropped and Dr Middleton observed that the mare's-tails were a good sign. The whole family went down the hundred yards to the beach, each one carrying something — a basket, a deckchair, a lilo.

'Where else in the world but Scotland would we have the beach to ourselves on a day like this?' said Mrs Middleton. The doctor agreed with a grunt. Michael got stripped to his swimming trunks and they taught Neil to play boule in the hard sand near the water. The balls were of bright grooved steel and he enjoyed trying to lob them different ways until he finally copied the doctor who showed him how to put back-spin on them. Anne wore a turquoise bikini and kept hooking her fingers beneath the elastic of her pants and snapping them out to cover more of her bottom. She did this every time she bent to pick up her boule and Neil came to watch for it. When they stopped playing Michael and his sister ran off to leap about in the breakers — large curling walls, glass-green, which nearly knocked them off their feet. From where he stood Neil could only hear their cries faintly. He went and sat down with the doctor and his wife.

'Do you not like the water?' she asked. She was lying on a sunbed, gleaming with suntan oil. She had her dress rucked up beyond her knees and her shoulder straps loosened.

'No. It's too cold.'

'The only place *I'll* ever swim again is the Med,' said the doctor.

'Sissy,' said his wife, without opening her eyes. Neil lay down and tried to think of a better reason for not swimming. His mother had one friend who occasionally phoned for her to go to the Commonwealth Pool. When she really didn't feel like it there was only one excuse that seemed to work.

At tea Michael took a perverse pleasure out of telling him again and again how warm the water was and Anne innocently agreed with him.

The next day was scorching hot. Even at breakfast time they could see the heat corrugating the air above the slabbed part of the garden.

'You *must* come in for a swim today, Fry. I'm boiled already,' said Michael.

'The forecast is twenty-one degrees,' said the doctor from behind his paper. Anne whistled in appreciation.

Neil's thighs were sticking to the plastic of his chair. He said, 'My mother forgot to pack my swimming trunks. I looked yesterday.'

Mrs Middleton, in a flowing orange dressing-gown, spoke over her shoulder from the sink. 'Borrow a pair of Michael's.' Before he could stop her she had gone off with wet hands in search of extra swimming trunks.

'Couldn't be simpler,' she said, setting a navy blue pair with white side panels on the table in front of Neil.

'I'll get mine,' said Michael and dashed to his room. Anne sat opposite Neil on the Formica kitchen bench-top swinging her legs. She coaxed him to come swimming, again looking into his eyes. He looked down and away from them.

45

'Come on, Neil. Michael's not much fun in the water.'

'The fact is,' said Neil, 'I've got my period.'

There was a long silence and a slight rustle of the *Scotsman* as Dr Middleton looked over the top of it. Then Anne half-slid, half-vaulted off the bench and ran out. Neil heard her make funny snorts in her nose.

'That's too bad,' said the doctor and got up and went out of the room shutting the door behind him. Neil heard Anne's voice and her father's, then he heard the bedroom door shut. He folded his swimming trunks and set them on the sideboard. Mrs Middleton gave a series of little coughs and smiled at him.

'Can I help you with the dishes?' he asked. There was something not right.

'Are you sure you're well enough?' she said smiling. Neil nodded and began to lift the cups from various places in the room. She washed and he dried with a slow thoroughness.

'Neil, nobody is going to force you to swim. So you can feel quite safe.'

Michael came in with his swimming gear in a roll under his arm.

'Ready, small Fry?'

'Michael, could I have a word? Neil, could you leave those bathing trunks back in Michael's wardrobe?'

On the beach the boys lay down on the sand. Michael hadn't spoken since they left the house. He walked in front, he picked the spot, he lay down and Neil followed him. The sun was hot and again they had the beach to themselves. Neil picked up a handful of sand and examined it as he spilled it out slowly.

'I bet you there's at least one speck of gold on this beach,' he said.

'That's a bloody stupid thing to say.'

'I'll bet you there is.'

Michael rolled over turning his back. 'I can pick them.'

'What?'

'I can really pick them.'

'What do you mean?'

'I might as well have asked a girl to come away on holiday.'

Neil's fist bunched in the sand.

'What's the use of somebody who won't go in for a dip?'

'I can't, that's all.'

'My Mum says you must have a very special reason. What is it, Fry?'

Neil opened his hand and some of the damp, deeper sand remained in little segments where he had clenched it. He was almost sure Anne had laughed.

'I'm not telling you.'

'Useless bloody Mama's boy,' said Michael. He got up flinging a handful of sand at Neil and ran down to the water. Some of the sand went into Neil's eyes, making him cry. He knuckled them clear and blinked, watching Michael jump, his elbows up, as each glass wave rolled at him belly-high.

Neil shouted hopelessly towards the sea. 'That's the last time I'm getting you into the pictures.'

He walked back towards the house. He had been here a night, a day and a morning. It would be a whole week before he could get home. Right now he felt he *was* a Mama's boy. He just wanted to climb the stair and be with her behind the closed door of their house. This had been the first time in his life he had been away from her and, although he had been reluctant because of this very thing, she had insisted that he could not turn down an invitation from the doctor's family. *It will teach you how to conduct yourself in good society.*

At lunch time Michael did not speak to him but made up salad rolls and took them on to the patio. Anne and her father had gone into the village on bicycles. Neil sat at the table chewing his roll with difficulty and staring in front of him. *If there is one thing I cannot abide it's a milk bottle on the table.* Mrs Middleton was the only one left for him to talk to.

'We met Mrs Wan this morning,' he said.

'Oh did you? She's a rum bird — feeding all those cats.'

'How many has she?'

'I don't know. They're never all together at the same time. She's a Duchess, you know?'

'A real one?'

'Yes. I can't remember her title — from somewhere in England. She married some Oriental and lived in the Far East. Africa too for a time. When he died she came home. Look.' She waved her hand at all the bric-à-brac. 'Look at this.' She went to a glass-fronted cabinet and took out what looked like a lace ball. It was made of ivory and inside was another ball with just as intricately carved mandarins and elephants and palm leaves, with another one inside that again.

'The question is how did they carve the one inside. It's all one piece.'

Neil turned it over in his hands marvelling at the mystery. He handed it carefully back.

'You wouldn't want to play boule with that,' he said.

'Isn't it exquisitely delicate?'

He nodded and said, 'Thank you for the lunch. It was very nourishing.'

He wandered outside in the garden and sat for a while by the pool. It was hot and the air was full of the noise of insects and bees moving in and out the flowers. He went down to the beach and saw that his friend Michael had joined up with some other boys to play cricket. He sat down out of sight of them at the side of a sand-dune. He lay back and closed his eyes. They had laughed at him in school when he said he didn't know what l.b.w. meant. He had been given a free cricket bat but there was hardly a mark on it because he couldn't seem to hit the ball. It was so hard and came at him so fast that he was more interested in getting out of its way than playing any fancy strokes. Scholarship boys were officially known as foundationers but the boys called them 'fundies' or 'fundaments'. When he asked what it meant somebody told him to look it up in a dictionary. 'Part of body on which one sits; buttocks; anus.'

He lifted his head and listened. At first he thought it was the noise of a distant seagull but it came again and he knew it wasn't. He looked up to the top of the sand-dune and saw a kitten, its tiny black tail upright and quivering.

'Pshhh-wshhh.'

He climbed the sand and lifted it. It miaowed thinly. He stroked its head and back and felt the frail fish bones of its ribs. It purred and he carried it back to the house. He climbed the steps behind the kitchen and saw a caravan screened by a thick hedge. The door was open and he had to hold it steady with his knee before he could knock on it.

'Come in,' Mrs Wan's voice called. Neil stepped up into the van. After the bright sunlight it was gloomy inside. It smelt of old and cat. He saw Mrs Wan sitting along one wall with her feet up.

'I found this and thought maybe it was yours,' said Neil handing the cat over to her. She scolded it.

'You little monkey,' she said and smiled at Neil. 'This cat is a black sheep. He's always wandering off. Thank you, young man. It was very kind of you to take the trouble to return him.'

'It was no trouble.'

She was dressed as she had been the day before except for the gloves. Her hands were old and her fingers bristled with rings. She waved at him as he turned to go.

'Just a minute. Would you like something to drink — as a reward?' She stood up and rattled in a cupboard above the sink.

'I think some tonic water is all I can offer you. Will that do?' She didn't give him a clean glass but just rinsed one for a moment under the thin trickle from the swan-neck tap at the tiny sink. She chased three cats away from the covered bench seat and waved him to sit down. Because the glass was not very clean the bubbles adhered to its sides. He saw that nothing was clean as he looked about the place. There were several tins of Kit-e-Kat opened on the draining-board and a silver fork encrusted with the stuff lay beside them. There were saucers all over the floor with milk which had evaporated in the heat leaving yellow rings. Everything was untidy. He set his glass between a pile of magazines and a marmalade pot on the table. She asked him his name and about his school and where he lived and about his father. Neil knew that his mother would call her nosey but he thought that she seemed interested in all his answers. She listened intently, blinking and staring at him with her face slightly turned as if she had a deaf ear.

'My father died a long time ago,' he said.

'And your mother?'

'She's alive.'

'And what does she do for a living?'

'She works in the cinema.' .

'Oh how interesting. Is she an actress?'

'No. She just works there. With a torch. She gets me in free — for films that are suitable for me. Sometimes I take my friend Michael with me.'

'Is that the boy below?'

'Yes.'

'I thought his name was Benjamin. But how marvellous that you can see all these films free.' She clapped her ringed hands together and seemed genuinely excited. 'I used to love the cinema. The cartoons were my favourite. And the newsreels. I'll bet you're very popular when a good picture comes to town.'

'Yes I am,' said Neil and smiled and sipped his tonic.

'Let's go outside and talk. It's a shame to waste such a day in here.' Neil offered his arm as she lowered herself from the step to the ground.

'What a polite young man.'

'That's my mother's fault.'

They sat on the deckchairs facing the sun and she lit a cigarette, holding it between her jewelled fingers. Her face was brown and criss-crossed with wrinkles.

'Why aren't you in swimming on such a day?' she asked.

Neil hesitated, then heard himself say, 'I can't. I've got a disease.'

'What is it?'

Again he paused but this old woman seemed to demand the truth.

'A thing — on my chest.'

'Let me see?' she said and leaned forward. He was amazed to find himself unbuttoning his shirt and showing her his mark. In the sunlight it didn't look so red. She scrutinized it and hummed, pursing her mouth and biting her lower lip.

'Why does it stop you bathing?'

Neil shrugged and began to button up when she stopped him.

'Let the sun at it. I'm sure it can do no harm.' He left his shirt lying open. 'When I was in Africa I worked with lepers.'

'Lepers?'

'Yes. So the sight of you doesn't worry me,' she said. 'Watch that you don't suffer from more than just the disease.'

'I don't understand.'

'It's bad enough having it without being shy about it as well.'

'Have you got leprosy now?'

'No. It's not as contagious as everybody says.'

Neil finished his tonic and lay back in the chair. The sun was bright and hot on his chest. He listened to Mrs Wan talking about leprosy, of how the lepers lost their fingers and toes, not because of the disease but because they had lost all feeling in them and they broke and damaged them without knowing. Eventually they got gangrene. Almost all the horrible things of leprosy, she said, were secondary. Suddenly he heard Michael's voice.

'Mrs Wan, Mum says could you tell her where . . .' his voice tailed off seeing Neil's chest, ' . . . the cheese grater is?'

'Do you know, I think I brought it up here.' She got up and stepped slowly into the caravan. Neil closed over his shirt and began to button it. Neither boy said a word.

At tea Michael spoke to him as if they were friends again and in bed that night it was Neil's suggestion that they go for a swim.

'Now? Are you mad?'

'They say it's warmer at night.'

'Yeah and we could make dummies in the beds like Clint Eastwood.'

'They don't *have* to look like Clint Eastwood.' They both laughed quiet sneezing laughs.

After one o'clock they dropped out of the window and ran to the beach. For almost half an hour in the pale darkness Neil thrashed and shivered. Eventually he sat down to wait in the warmer shallows, feeling the withdrawing sea hollow the sand around him. Further out, Michael whooped and rode the breakers like a shadow against their whiteness.

In the Hills above Lugano

I had first met Brendan through the Debating Society when he was a mature student at University doing medicine. I liked his moroseness, his intelligence and his drinking habits — which were much the same as mine at the time. We had been, despite the ten-year age difference, reasonably friendly. But it was with some surprise that I read his invitation to spend a week of the summer holiday with him and his wife in a place he had acquired for a month near Lugano in Switzerland.

'It'll be a reunion in the sun,' he wrote.

I really didn't know him all that well — but money for a provincial publisher is scarce and I had not had a real holiday for several years.

He met me off the train and his first words were, 'On a point of information?'

'What?'

'How are you, young fella?' He shook my hand with both of his, then put his arm around my shoulder on the way to the car. It is disconcerting to find that an acquaintance considers you his best friend, his soul mate, but I could do nothing about it. He was in good form and as we drove up into the hills above Lugano he kept smiling and shaking his head in disbelief.

'How many years is it?' he said.

'Five — six?'

'It's ten.'

'I don't believe you.'

'And we all swore we'd meet up again every year. The best laid plans — blah-blah.'

'Hey, this is some place.' The scenery was magnificent — dry ochre hills covered with trees and dense foliage, lakes lying blue in the hazy distance.

'This is my wife, Linden,' he said. She was a tall girl, young for him — about the same age as myself — with a wisp-like quality of beauty about her. She wore a simple white dress and her skin was a golden brown from the first fortnight of the holiday.

'Hi,' she said and looked away from me shyly.

We ate on the patio and continued to sit at the table and drink the very excellent local wine until darkness fell. At one point, when Brendan went off to get another bottle from the fridge, Linden leaned over and said to me, 'I'm glad you're here. He's been so down of late. Utterly, utterly black moods. You're the only one he's ever talked to me about.'

The fireflies came out, icy points of blue light, and flitted in the hot darkness. They hovered in one place for a moment then skidded off to another. Crickets kept up a constant trilling noise.

'How's the publishing?' Brendan asked.

'We've a very good Autumn list coming.'

'The last novel got excellent reviews.'

'I thought the author and I were the only ones who read those.'

'We keep abreast. No philistines here.'

'No,' said Linden. 'I admire what you're doing — and having the courage to publish poetry.'

'It doesn't take courage — just money.'

Later Brendan became nostalgic, inevitably talking about people whom Linden didn't know. I was aware that she was withdrawing from the conversation, her eyes straying away to look into the night or follow the path of a firefly. Brendan recalled our sessions together with a clarity I did not think was possible.

'Do you remember that afternoon in Hannigan's?'

I nodded. I could recall the bar and having been in it once or twice but had no recollection of being there with Brendan.

'And you made the statement that there was no such thing as an unselfish act.'

'Did I?'

He went on to outline my arguments from the past, the amounts we drank, who was in the company. It had obviously meant a great deal more to him than to me. And as he talked occasionally Linden caught me looking at her and once she smiled.

The next morning I awoke with a sore head. I felt dishevelled and awful as I made my way down to breakfast in my dressing-gown. Linden was sunbathing on her stomach at the side of the small pool, writing in a loose-leaf folder. When she noticed me she put on her bikini top and got up to make me coffee.

'I can do it,' I said. But she insisted. I think she was conscious of me looking at her because when she brought a pot of coffee and some croissants to the table she had put on an orange towelling beach robe.

'Did we talk rubbish last night?'

She smiled but did not answer.

'Where's Brendan?'

'Still abed.'

She sat down at the table, the perfume of her suntan oil wafting towards me. Just then a small middle-aged man in a navy T-shirt came across the patio. Looking neither right nor left he went down the three steps to the pool. He walked slowly, dragging his heels.

'Who's that?'

'He owns the place. Lives in a hut at the back during the summer.'

The man took a long pole with a net on it and skimmed some flower petals and leaves from the surface of the pool. He clattered the pole back in its place and left the same way he had come, paying no attention whatsoever to us.

'What a gloomy wee man.'

'Money makes some people miserable. He doesn't look like he'd own a place like this.'

'But . . . we're on our holidays.' I poured myself another coffee. 'Where did you two meet?'

'In a hospital in Toronto.' She smiled. 'I was visiting and he ran after me — the whole way up the corridor — and said, "I'm looking for an excuse to talk to you but I can't think of one."'

'He was always a smooth talker.'

'No, he really meant it. But I agree, the way he spoke was really neat.'

'And what did you do . . . before Brendan?'

'Anything, everything. I'd been to college and graduated. Drama. I'd modelled a bit. I went to LA and tried to get into the movies. I was screen-tested for *Alien*.'

'Really?'

'Yes. But Sigourney Weaver got the part.'

'Did you try for others?'

'It was then I met Brendan. I had to make decisions.' She laughed. 'He won.'

'Speak of the devil.'

Brendan appeared in bathing trunks, muttered a good morning and plunged into the pool.

Later he and I walked down to the supermarket while Linden got on with her sunbathing. The villa was at the end of a leafy lane and Brendan pulled a switch from the hedge as he walked. He deleafed it and whipped it about.

He talked about his research — he was working on the effects of certain inhaled gases on brain tissue — and managed to explain, even to me, some of the complexities and problems.

'I work on rats, of course.'

'Are their brains the same?'

'Elements are.'

'Who'd be a rat? Made to sniff your gases — brain damage — then killed to be examined?'

'It's for our good eventually.'

'I suppose so.' The air was hot and I was conscious of moving through it. 'Ahhh — this heat is wonderful,' I said.

'Wait until midday. Linden and I have taken to the siesta habit. It's all you can do when it's that hot.'

55

I raised an eyebrow. He whipped the switch across my backside.

'I didn't mean that, you adolescent.'

Because of my good Italian Brendan let me do all the transactions in the supermarket. After we had loaded a bag with groceries he said, 'Is it too early for a cure?'

'Why not?'

We sat outside on the patio of a small restaurant and ordered a bottle of white. The glasses when they were filled turned opaque with the coldness of the wine.

'You're getting a gut, Doctor,' I said. He slapped his paunch loudly.

'I am the age to wear it.'

'Linden is very beautiful.'

'Yes, I know.' His voice was quiet. He reached out with his stick and drew the point of it down the side of the glass, making a clear track in the condensation. Then he said, 'We've been brought up wrongly to deal with sexuality. Dogs have it right. And doctors.'

I waited for him to elaborate.

'A doctor meets a beautiful woman in his surgery and before you can say knife he has her stripped and lying down. A minute later he's palpated her breasts and sunk his finger in every available orifice. After that he can get to know her. That kind of thing should be socially compulsory. Dogs have it right. "I'd like you to meet Miss O'Neill," and instead of shaking hands you have a good look and a rummage between her legs and a good sniff. Get the trivial things out of the way first.'

'That's a bitter Swiftian vision. Not one that appeals to me.'

Brendan shrugged and bent his switch in an arc until it broke. 'A green-stick fracture,' he said and dropped it on the floor.

'It's got to be more beautiful than that. More spiritual.'

He laughed.

'It always amuses me when people make spiritual claims for the most *physical* of all human acts.'

'I don't want to be personal but does Linden agree with you about this?'

'We don't talk about it. This is why I'm so glad to see you.

We can say anything to each other. Between friends nothing is barred.'

Brendan slugged off what was left in his glass and refilled it. I did not know what to say to his assumption of our closeness.

'For Christsake, why should we associate physical beauty with sexuality — it's not even physical beauty but a perfection of averageness. None of your black women with broad noses or fat Renoir nudes nowadays. They have to conform to the soft porn magazine. Fuck me, what crassness! What a load of fuckin baloney!'

I felt uncomfortable and tried to change the subject. The thought of Brendan in one of his utterly black moods for the rest of the holiday scared me. I suggested another bottle.

'Why not,' he said.

'Linden tells me she nearly got into films.'

He looked at me askance. 'An extra. She tried to get taken on as an extra in *Alien*.'

'There were no extras in *Alien*. It was all set on a spaceship.'

'Maybe it was *Reds*, then. There were thousands of extras in that.'

'You don't encourage her much.'

'It all exists in here with Linden.' He tapped his temple. I didn't like to probe any further but smiled down at my white knees.

We finished the second bottle between us and returned to the villa. Linden put her arm round Brendan's thickening waist and they went off for a siesta. In my room I slept almost immediately after the wine. When I woke I heard a strange noise — it must have been Linden — a kind of suppressed whimpering. Hissing whispers. Afterwards when they came down to the poolside there seemed to be nothing amiss and he laughed at some joke she had made. But she would not repeat it for me.

In the evening when Brendan was preparing the meal Linden and I sat on the patio drinking Camparis. Brendan's voice floated out into the night imitating a French tenor, singing 'Pour un baiser'.

'Do you see how good you are for him,' said Linden.

I nodded, unable to think of anything to say. The ice clicked and cracked in my glass. Her initial shyness of me seemed to have gone. She looked at me and her eyes held for longer than they should. I was unable to return her gaze and bowed my head. When I raised it again her eyes were still there – dark and beautiful – fixed on me. I called in to Brendan in the kitchen, 'Anything I can do to help?'

The next morning was very much the same as the first two. I went down to the pool in my dressing-gown and Linden was stretched out on a sunbed with her ring binder open on the ground in front of her. But she was asleep. I went over to her and before I cleared my throat I could not resist looking at her. I could see the wonderful length of her brown back, the side of her breast where it pressed softly against the sunbed. Her black hair was up to let the sun at her shoulders. I tried to tiptoe away but suddenly she wakened.

'Hi,' she said and smiled. She put on her top and sat up, flicking her hair back.

'What's the file?'

'Something I'm working on.'

'Like?'

'A screenplay.'

'I've never seen one of those. May I?'

'You of all people. No. I'd be embarrassed. It has no shape to it yet. Let me get you some coffee.'

'No. Let *me* get *you* some – for a change.'

We sat and talked for about an hour, drinking our way down a whole pot of coffee. I discovered that she and Brendan weren't actually married.

'It seems the easiest thing to say. We've been together for about eighteen months now. I needed the protection of one person – a moat if you like.'

'From?'

'From being hounded. I was getting into a lot of bad emotional relationships.' She indicated her body with her spread hands as if to explain. 'Every man I met wanted me on my back.' I stared at my knees which had turned pink from yesterday. Somewhere in the house a door slammed.

'The top of the marning, to yis,' said Brendan and he strode between us to dive into the pool. When he surfaced, blowing like a whale, he shouted, 'That kitchen's beginning to stink.'

I offered to help Linden and she asked me to take the rubbish down to the bin. I tied two bulging black bags which, by the smell coming from them, were a risk to our health and took them down the steps to the side of the house. The man in the navy T-shirt came round the corner with a similar black bag tied at the neck. We were too close for him to have ignored me.

'*Buon giorno,*' I said. He nodded. I wondered if he had some disease or an eye infection because his face was streaming with tears.

'*Cosa di male?*' I asked him, when I realized he was simply crying. He sniffed and rubbed his forearm across his face, said it was nothing. I held the heavy lid of the drum open for him and he thanked me. When I let it slam into place he told me that it was an anniversary for him. He took out a handkerchief and wiped his mouth and eyes. This day twelve years ago, he said, a terrible thing had happened. His only daughter had been murdered. Just walking in the hills above Lugano. They never got the man who did it. She was just twenty years of age. Just beginning her life. I stood there, my hands empty, trying to make sense of his oddly-accented Italian. Why does that kind of thing happen? You sound like an intelligent man. Tell me.

'*Peccato . . . peccato . . .* I'm sorry,' was all I could think of. He turned muttering to himself and walked away from me. Had I made a mistake — taken him up wrongly? When I told Brendan and Linden about the conversation Brendan just shrugged.

'He might be telling the truth. Who knows? Anyway, we were all canning peas outside Spalding.' He laughed but Linden was obviously disturbed by the story because she barely spoke a word all afternoon.

In the early hours of the morning I awoke and, as sometimes happens when I have had too much to drink, could not get back to sleep again. Eventually I got up to go to the lavatory. The window, which overlooked the pool, was open and insects hummed and fluttered round the light bulb. I looked out and saw the pale figure of Brendan squatting beside the pool. He was totally naked. My eyes were attracted to the knot of gristle

59

and hair between his thighs. He was hunkered down, staring at the lit glassy pane of turquoise water. Even from this distance I could see the blackness in his eyes which did not move but seemed hypnotically riveted on the surface or in the depths of the water. Occasionally he flicked his hanging penis with his fingers the way another man would touch his moustache or adjust his glasses on the bridge of his nose. For some reason I directed my stream quietly down the side of the bowl and did not flush the toilet after me.

I could not sleep and read a Moravia from my bedside shelf for an hour or so until dawn. I don't know whether it was curiosity or another call of nature made me go to the lavatory again but Brendan was still there in the milky morning light. He had changed his position and now sat on the side of the pool with his feet dangling in the water. But his eyes stared in the same fashion, looking at nothing and at everything.

The next night at dinner Brendan drank heavily and was argumentative and objectionable. Both Linden and I were constantly putting our hands over our glasses as he poured glass after glass of wine for himself. It was a very hot night and I could see the sweat standing out on his face the more he drank. At the coffee stage he produced my gift of duty-free Irish whiskey and poured himself a tumblerful. And another. The crickets kept up their calls like unanswered phones in the woods.

'Do you write a screenplay with a specific actress in mind?'

Brendan sniggered and I looked at him but he didn't say anything.

'No,' said Linden. 'You can think of the best actress. If you write the character well, the actress should be able to make it believable.'

'De Niro ... Streep ... Fonda ... Jack Nicholson,' Brendan listed the names punctuated by snorts of laughter. Linden ignored him and because she was talking directly to me I had to do the same.

'How do you know how to set about it?'

'There was a section on my drama course. My course tutor said I handled it well.'

'I'll bet he did,' said Brendan. He laughed and slammed the table with his hand so that the spoons rang. Linden looked at me and began to bite her thumb-nail. Brendan poured himself another very large whiskey and sipped it noisily.

'Can I ask what is it about?'

Linden shrugged. She picked up a piece of card and began to fan herself. The motion wafted her perfume towards me.

'It's about a woman who's trying to come to terms with herself and her life. She started out as a beautician then got into the manufacturing side of make-up. It's the irony of the outside and the inside. And how she copes with success.'

'Sounds interesting.'

'Why . . . WHY', shouted Brendan, 'don't you write about something you KNOW about? Fuck success. Why don't you write about failure, Linden. Eh? Failure with a capital F?'

She did not turn her head to him but kept staring out into the darkness. Tears came into her eyes but she quickly blinked them away.

'You're drunk,' she said. 'Go to bed.'

'Ah-ha, you've rumbled me.' He began to sing, 'Noo-bod-ee loves like an Irishman.' He swung his arms wide and toppled an empty wine bottle. It smashed among our feet on the stone floor of the patio.

'GO TO BED.' Linden's voice was tight with anger. They got up simultaneously as if they were about to come to blows but Linden went to get a brush and Brendan bounced off the jamb of the door and staggered across the room to the stairs.

I sat on the chair and listened to the empty echoing sound of broken glass being thrown in the bucket. Linden came back and lowered herself into her chair.

'I'm sorry about this.'

'Not to worry.'

'It must be very embarrassing for you. To have to sit and talk to your friend's wife.'

'Actually I feel more relaxed now that he's gone.'

'I think I deserve a drink,' she said. In the American fashion she filled her glass with ice-cubes then poured herself a whiskey. She pointed the bottle at me and I nodded. When she sat again she put the cold glass to her forehead.

'It's so warm tonight.' The fireflies flicked out beyond the lights of the pool. 'I so hate him when he's like that.'

'Drink changes some people.'

'Please, don't talk about him.' She rearranged her long legs and tucked one heel up underneath her. 'Tell me about publishing.'

'What about it?'

'Finding someone new. That must be exciting.'

'Yes, it is. But if they're any good they move on to a big London house.'

'I've written a novel – a short one.'

'Really?'

'It's been rejected by lots of publishers back home in the States. One of them was kind enough to say it would make a good screenplay. That's what I'm working on at the moment.'

I began to wonder if, at last, I'd discovered why Brendan had invited me. Had she coaxed him? I wiped the perspiration from my forehead with the bottom of my shirt.

'Would you like me to read the novel?'

'It's very kind of you to offer but . . . no. I think I see its faults now.'

'What's it called?'

'I'm sorry I brought it up. Can we just leave it?'

She swirled her ice-cubes in her glass and drained off her drink.

'Too long for a title.' She smiled and stood.

'I think', she said, 'I'm going to swim. Do you want to join me?'

'Okay.' She stood up, her hands reached down to the hem of her dress and with one sweeping movement she pulled it off over her head, shaking her hair loose as she did so. She was wearing only the briefest of white underwear. She skipped away as if she was shy or modest and dived into the pool.

'I'll be down in a moment,' I said. Upstairs I had some difficulty in getting into my bathing trunks and it didn't help to hear Brendan's heavy snores from the bedroom. I had just come out on to the patio when I heard her scream. She threshed towards the edge of the pool making a kind of whinnying noise.

'What is it? What's wrong?' She pulled herself up on straightened arms, sat on the side and winced.

'Something . . . an insect . . . huge . . . ' I looked and saw in the lights of the pool what looked like a grasshopper with whirring wings. But it was the size of a big, fat cigar.

'It's horrible. It hit me in the face.' She was still shuddering with nausea at the thought of it. I reached for the pole with the net and captured the thing and pulled it nearer to inspect it.

'It's a locust, by God.'

'Kill it. It's horrible.'

'If you think I'm putting my bare foot on that . . . '

I sank the net and held the insect under the water. Its elbows and knees made frantic rowing motions and its wings twitched. My dry shoulder was touching Linden's wet one as she tried to see into the net.

'It must have come millions of miles,' I said. 'Thought you only got them in Africa.'

'Hold it under for five minutes,' said Linden. She put her wet arm on my back and I flinched.

'You're wet.' Coming out of the water her underwear had become almost transparent and I kept looking away, or at least looking at her face. I toppled forward into the pool and began to swim up and down.

'This is lovely.'

'I'm not going in with that thing there,' she said. She went up the steps and poured two more drinks and brought them down to the poolside. She was drying her hair when I got out.

'Is this for me?' She nodded and drank a little of her own. I lifted the net and saw no movement from the creature. 'Stone dead.' I sat down beside her on the sun-bed.

'Be careful with the glass on the patio. In your bare feet,' she said. 'I'll do it properly tomorrow.'

I kissed her, lightly at first — in a friendly fashion almost. She responded and kissed me with passion. She was like a coiled spring, full of unexpected jumps and starts. When I touched her breasts she gritted her teeth and tensed.

'What's wrong?' I could barely speak.

'I keep expecting pain. Brendan likes to . . . he hurts me.'

At the mention of his name I drew away from her. She sat with her hands between her knees and her head bowed.

'I'm sorry,' she said. Suddenly there was a whirring, chattering noise at our feet as the locust lurched out of the net.

Linden screamed again and it took to the air, throbbing like some machine, and disappeared into the dark.

'It's gone. It's okay now,' I said, putting my arms around her shoulders. I tried to kiss her again but she tucked her chin into her shoulder. I kissed her arms and shoulders. I was shaking now.

'I love you,' she said. 'Have done since the day you arrived.'

'You're one of the most beautiful women I've ever met. I cannot believe I am so close to you.' She allowed me to kiss her again. 'He's asleep. I heard him snoring.'

'We'll go to your room. There's a lock on the door.' Linden did not put on her dress again but tiptoed up the stairs in front of me with it draped over her shoulder. I was relieved to hear that Brendan had stopped his snoring.

Throughout our love-making she kept saying over and over again, 'You're so gentle.' When it was finished she said once more that she loved me.

'I want you to take me away from him.' There was a long silence between us.

'Is it that serious?'

'Your friend . . . is . . . My pain is the only thing that arouses him.'

'Brendan? That's hard to believe.'

'You haven't been to bed with him.'

'True.'

'In the beginning it was fine . . . but now he has to . . . he brings things home from the hospital . . . '

'Like what?'

She turned her face away from me. Her lips moved but no sound came out.

'I can't begin to understand that.' I was tracing out her body with my fingers. Soon the talk stopped and we made love again. I tried to persuade her that this was a night we could both cherish in our memories – a photograph, – a searing flash – but again she said, 'I love you. I want to go away with you.'

It was four o'clock when she left my room, quietly unsnibbing the door. Almost immediately I heard voices in the corridor. Brendan must have seen her coming from my room in that half-clothed state. I lay there naked and nervous wondering what I could do. A toilet flushed and Brendan's heavier footsteps came to my door. He pushed it open and stood there, still fully-dressed.

'Hi,' I said. He looked at me and slowly tapped the side of his temple.

'It all happens in there with Linden. Remember that.' Then he was away.

I could not sleep, of course. I remembered people in Zurich whose address I could get from the telephone book. At five I began to pack and as the dawn came up I was going quietly down the stairs. I left them a brief thank you note on the kitchen table. Outside it was already warm and the birds were singing. I looked back at the villa and saw the owner in his navy T-shirt sitting at the window of his hut. I felt I had to wave to him and he answered by raising his hand in a kind of tired salute.

End of Season

The elder Miss Bradley walked to the end of the small pier and stood listening to the sea thumping in from below. White horses flecked the bay and the wind was strong enough to make her avert her face from its direction. She was convinced that the summer was over. A week back at school and already the first gale of winter. On this exposed coast with no trees autumn did not exist.

She liked to come here on her way home, particularly on windy days. It rinsed the experience of school from her. She did not stand long — a minute, perhaps two, facing into the wind with her eyes closed. Then she turned on her heel and walked slowly, leaning back into the wind, trying not to let its strength fluster her or make her movements awkward.

The briefcase was heavy with jotters and she wished she had brought the car. The school was only three-quarters of a mile from the house but each day she debated whether or not she should walk the distance for the good of her health. It would not do to have two invalids in the one house.

The family home was one of a terrace of cream-painted houses, set back from the road behind long, well-kept gardens. Some of the houses still had little gibbets overhanging the pavement with 'Bed & Breakfast' signs swinging in the wind. As she walked up the path she faintly heard her sister, Kathleen, laughing and thought it odd — a feeling which increased when she opened the front door and smelt tobacco smoke. In the front room a man sat in her armchair beside the bookcase, with his back to the light, talking.

'Ah Mary, there you are,' said her sister. The man stood up politely.

'You remember Mr Maguire?'

'Eh . . . yes, indeed.'

In his hand Mr Maguire held their old guest book. He sat down again and opened it so quickly that he must have had his finger in the place. 'I was just looking at when we were here last.' He passed the book to Mary. She found Mr and Mrs Maguire whose stay was dated July 1958.

'We were on our honeymoon,' he said. 'We had only booked one night but we stayed a week.' The man had a distinct Belfast accent.

'Mr Maguire thought we were still a guest house,' said Kathleen.

'Oh no. We stopped that a long time ago.' Mary flicked to the last entry in the book. 'In 1971.' She set it on the sideboard and, rubbing her hands, moved closer to the fire.

'It's like January,' she said. 'Is the kettle on?'

Her sister asked Mr Maguire if he would have more tea.

'I wouldn't say no.' He handed over his empty cup and saucer and Kathleen rattled it on to the tray with her own. She elbowed her way out of the door to the kitchen, leaving Mary and the stranger in silence.

'Are you looking for a place to stay?' Mary asked.

'Yes. I decided to treat myself to a holiday. It's years since I've gone anywhere.'

'Have you tried any of the other guest houses?'

'No. This is where I wanted to come.'

'It was nice of you to remember us.'

'It's funny how well you remember good times, holidays,' he said. 'I'm sure you don't remember us. We would have been one couple in a crowded summer.'

'Yes, sometimes it's difficult. But I rarely forget a face. Names, yes.'

Mary sat down on the rug in a delicate side-saddle posture and shivered. From her low position she could see the man's immaculately polished shoes. Her mother had always told her a man's footwear was the key to his character. 'Beware of someone with dirty shoes,' she had said. 'Even worse is the man who has polished his shoes but neglected to do his heels. But worst of all is the man with black polish stains on his socks. It's the ultimate sloth.' Mary looked up at him but his face was in shadow because his back was to the grey light from the window. He wore an open-necked shirt, a pair of trousers too light for his age and a blue sweater with a small emblem of a red jaguar on it.

'And Mrs Maguire?'

'My wife died last December.'

'Oh I'm sorry.'

'She had been ill for a long time. It was a merciful release.'

'Oh I am sorry,' she said. 'What brings you back to this part of the world?' He hesitated before answering.

'I wanted to see Spanish Point. Where the galleon went down. *The Girona*.'

'Yes, I walk out there frequently myself. There's nothing much. Rocks, sea.'

'I was at an exhibition in the museum − of the stuff they brought up − and I thought I'd just like to look at the place. Imagine it a bit.'

Kathleen's voice called loudly from the kitchen. Mary excused herself and went out.

'He wants to stay for a couple of nights,' whispered Kathleen. 'I told him I'd have to ask you. What do you think?'

'How do you feel about it? Can you cope?'

'Yes, I don't mind. The money would come in handy.' Mary was about to go back to the other room when her sister held her by the arm.

'But listen to this,' Kathleen laughed and wheezed. 'We had been talking about books. He tells me he reads a lot − as a matter of fact he's book mad − and when I came in with the tea I said "Do you like Earl Grey?" and he says, "I don't know. What did he write?" Isn't that marvellous?' Mary smiled and nodded while Kathleen giggled uncontrollably, saying to herself, 'Stop it Kathleen,' and slapping the back of her wrist. She straightened her face and set out some more biscuits on a plate. Then she burst out laughing again.

'He kept talking about the eedgit, at one stage.'

'The what?'

'The book "The Eedgit". One of the big Russians. He meant *The Idiot*.'

'Oh,' said Mary.

'Really, Kathleen, control yourself.' Her sister again straightened her face and picked up the tray. Mary opened the door for her.

'It'll be something for me to do,' Kathleen whispered over her shoulder as she led the way into the other room.

'That'll be fine, Mr Maguire,' she said. 'If you'll give me a minute I'll fix up your room for you.' He edged forward in his seat and made a vague gesture as if to assist Kathleen with the tray.

'Thank you very much,' he said and smiled up at the two sisters. 'I'll try and cause as little disruption as possible.' Mary sat on the rug again to be near the fire. Mr Maguire sipped from his cup holding his saucer close to his chest.

'Why did you stop the bed and breakfast?' he asked.

'Several reasons,' said Kathleen. 'Me for one. My asthma was getting intolerable. It's really a nervous condition with me. The very thought of summer would bring on an attack. Then there was the Troubles, of course. After 'sixty-nine people just stopped coming. Now we call this place the last resort.'

'When we were here the place was full of Scotch.'

'Yes, and the same ones came back year after year. But after the Troubles started nobody would risk it. Then Mary got a job teaching when the new school was built.'

'And mother died,' said Mary.

'Oh did she? I never saw her. We just heard her – upstairs.'

'She was very demanding,' said Kathleen, 'and I was in no position to cope with her. It was she really who insisted that we keep the place open. All her life she had a great fear of ending up in the poor-house. She was the one who had the bright idea of extending out the back just before the slump. We're still paying the mortgage.'

Mr Maguire set his cup and saucer on the hearth. 'Do you mind if I smoke a pipe?' He addressed Mary who turned to her sister.

'Kathleen?'

'I like the smell of pipe-smoke. It's cigarettes I can't stand.'

Mr Maguire took out a small pipe and a yellow plastic

pouch. He filled the pipe as he listened to Kathleen talk about the old days when the house was full of guests. Mary watched him press the tobacco into the bowl with his index finger. When he struck the match he whirled his hand in a little circle to attenuate the flare before holding the match to his pipe. The triangular flame gave little leaps as he held it over the bowl and drew air through it, his lips popping quietly. Throughout the whole operation he continued to nod and say 'hm-hm' to Kathleen's talk.

'You'll just have to take us as we are,' she was saying, 'not being officially open and all that. I'll give you a key and you can come and go as you like.'

'Thank you,' said Mr Maguire, striking another match.

'And breakfast. Would you like a fry in the morning?'

'Yes, please. It's the only time I ever do have the big fry. I wouldn't think I was on holiday if I didn't. Do you still bake your own wheaten bread?'

'No. My asthma. The flour can sometimes go for it. Let me get you an ashtray,' said Kathleen, jumping up. Mr Maguire sat with a tiny bouquet of dead matches between his fingers.

'Did you ever think of selling?'

Kathleen laughed and Mary smiled down at the fire.

'We tried for three years,' said Kathleen. 'Would you want to buy it? The ads were costing us so much that we had to take it off the market.'

When the tea was finished Kathleen showed him up to his room, talking constantly, even over her shoulder on the stairs. Mary followed them, her hands tucked into opposite sleeves, like a nun. The bed was stripped to its mattress of blue and white stripes. Mr Maguire set his bag by the window.

'I'll put the electric blanket on to air the bed for you,' said Kathleen.

'Thank you,' he said. 'You get a great view from this window.' Mary stared over his shoulder at the metallic sea. His face in the light was sallow and worn, with vertical creases down each side of his mouth and his forehead corrugated into wrinkles as he spoke. He wouldn't win any prizes for his looks but somehow his face suited him. He gave the impression of being an ex-sportsman, wiry and tough, sufficiently tall to have developed a slight stoop of the shoulders. He had enough hair to make her wonder whether or not it was a toupee. If it was it was a very convincing one.

'Where's a good place to eat now?'

'The Royal do a nice meal,' said Kathleen.

'The Royal?'

'Is that too expensive?'

'It was in my day.'

Kathleen lifted the foot of the bed and eased it out from the wall.

'Try the Croft Kitchen,' she said. 'I think they're still open. What little season there is, is over.' Seeing him hesitate she added, 'It's on High Street opposite what used to be the Amusements.' She stepped out on to the landing. 'The bathroom is second on your right. The light switch is on the outside.'

'Yes, I remember.'

'I'll just get some bed-linen.' Kathleen hurried off.

'She's excited,' said Mary, her voice lowered. Mr Maguire smiled and nodded. His voice was as quiet as hers.

'On our honeymoon,' he said, 'my wife went to the bathroom . . . ' Mary withdrew her hands from her sleeves and straightened a picture, ' . . . and someone turned out the light on her. She was terrified. She heard a footstep, then the light went out, then breathing. The poor woman sat for half the night in the dark before she had the courage to come out. I was sound asleep, of course.'

'How awful,' said Mary.

Kathleen strode in, the fresh bed-linen pressed between her arms like a white accordion. 'Right, there's work to be done,' she said, dumping them on the bed.

That night even though she felt tired and had gone to bed early Mary could not sleep. She heard Mr Maguire come in at a reasonable hour. Apart from a little throat-clearing he himself was quiet but she heard everything he did – the popping of the wash-hand basin in her own room as he used his, the flush of the toilet from the end of the corridor, through the wall the creaking of his bed as he got into it. It seemed hours before she heard the snap of his bedside light being switched off and she wondered what book it was that kept him reading so late.

She woke several times and each time was wet with perspiration, so much so that she was afraid she had had an accident. She felt like the shamelessly vulgar girl on the calendar which hung above the cash desk in the garage, emerging from the waves in a dripping white chemise which concealed nothing. Her condition was becoming worse instead of better. At times in front of her classes she felt as if there was a hole in her head and she was being filled from top to toe, like a hot-water bottle. Some months ago Kathleen had become alarmed seeing her sister steady herself with her knuckles on the kitchen table, her face red and wet with perspiration.

'What's wrong?'

Mary had simply said that her ovaries were closing down. The inner woman was giving up the ghost, but not without a struggle. She showered twice a day now – when she got up in the morning and before her evening meal. She refused to go to the doctor because, she said, the condition was normal. The *Home Encyclopedia of Medicine* told her all she wanted to know. Letters in women's magazins frequently dealt with the subject, in some cases in embarrassing detail. It was a sign of the times when you bought a perfectly middle-of-the-road woman's magazine and were frightened to open the pages because of what you might read: sex mixed in with the knitting patterns; among the recipes, orgasms and homosexuality and God knows what. She was embarrassed, not on her own behalf but for the teenagers in her classes. Magazines like the ones she bought would inevitably be going into all their homes. Each time her eyes flinched away from reading such an article she blushed for the destruction of her pupils' innocence. As for some of the daily papers, she wouldn't give them house-room.

Mr Maguire cleared his throat and she heard the twang of him turning in his seldom-used bed.

During the last class of the day Mary stood staring, not out, but at the window. On this the leeward side of the school, the glass was covered with rain droplets which trembled at each gust of wind. Behind her a fourth-year class worked quietly at a translation exercise. She was proud of her reputation for having the most disciplined classes in the school. She knew the pupils disliked her for it but it was something they would thank her for in later life.

At ten to four she saw Mr Maguire walking out of town with his hands clasped behind his back and his head down into the wind. When she eventually got out of school he was standing smiling at the gate.

'I thought it must be that time,' he said, 'and I was just passing.' He offered to carry her bag but she said that it was light enough. They began walking into the fine drizzle.

'What a day that was. Do you have children, Mr Maguire?'

'No, my wife was never a well woman. It would have been too much to ask.' Again she was struck by the coarseness of his accent. His face relaxed and he smiled. 'Where did all the books come from in your house?' he asked.

'That was my father mostly. He was Headmaster of the local Primary. He was interested in all sorts of things. Nature study, science, history. We were always used to books in the house.'

'Lucky. I had to do all the work myself. At a very late stage. Imagine sitting your A-levels for the first time at fifty.'

'Is that what you did?'

'I'm afraid so.'

'I admire that.'

Mr Maguire shrugged shyly.

'Not everybody does. My wife used to make fun of me. But she had a very hard time. She was in a lot of pain and couldn't understand. I think she was jealous of the time I spent reading. She thought it was a hobby or a pastime or something like that. She couldn't have been further from the truth.' Seeing Mary change her briefcase from her right to her left hand Mr Maguire insisted that he carry it. She reluctantly let him take it.

He continued talking. 'When you find out about real education you can never leave it alone. I don't mean A-levels and things like that — you are just proving something to yourself with them — but books, ideas, feelings. Everything to do with up here.' He tapped his temple. 'And here.' He tapped the middle of his chest.

Mary asked, 'What do you like to read then?'

'The classics. Fiction. Good stuff.'

The wind tugged at his hair, blowing it into various partings. It was definitely not a toupee.

'I sometimes stop here and walk to the end.' She pointed to the pier, its back arched against the running sea. Occasionally a wave broke over it and spray slapped down on the concrete. Some boys with school-bags were running the gauntlet along the pier.

'They'll get soaked, or worse,' said Mr Maguire.

'That's nothing. This summer I saw them ride off the end on a bicycle. They had it tied to one of the bollards so's they could pull it up each time. I couldn't watch. It gave me the funniest feeling. I had to go away in the end.'

When they got back to the house Mr Maguire set her briefcase in the hall, nodded to her and climbed the stairs. Mary went to the kitchen and sat on a stool beside the Rayburn drying out as the kettle boiled.

'Where's our guest?' asked Kathleen.

'Upstairs.'

'He's a strange fish. But nice.'

'Yes, you and he certainly seem to get along,' said Mary. Kathleen rolled her eyes to heaven.

Mary laughed and said, 'He walks like the Duke of Edinburgh.' She stood up and did an imitation backwards and forwards across the kitchen, her hands joined behind her back, her head forward like a tortoise.

Kathleen giggled, saying, 'I was making his bed today and do you know what he's reading? Or at least has lying on his bedside table.'

'I've no idea.'

'A book of English verse.'

'Why not?'

'It doesn't tally somehow. Him and poetry. And do you know — he's brought a full shoe-polishing kit with him. Brushes, tins, cloths, the lot. Mother would have been so pleased.'

'You shouldn't nosey.'

'I couldn't help seeing them. I had to move them out of the way to make the bed.'

'What's wrong with being careful about your appearance?'

'Nothing. But it does seem a bit extravagant.'

Kathleen heard Mr Maguire's footsteps on the landing and bounded to the kitchen door.

'There's a cup of tea in the pot, Mr Maguire,' she called.

When he came in Mary smelt soap off his hands as he reached in front of her for his cup.

'Well, how was your day?' asked Kathleen.

'The rain drove me home,' he smiled. His hair was dark and neatly parted, as if he had used hair-oil. 'You see how I call it home already.' Kathleen offered him a biscuit but he refused.

'How was your meal in the Croft Kitchen last night?'

'It was closed.'

'Where did you eat then?'

'The café on the front. It was good. Reasonable too.'

'Eucch, what a place,' Kathleen shuddered. 'All those sauce bottles on the tables. They're encrusted.'

'No, it was fine, really.'

'Look, we don't eat extravagantly ourselves but you're welcome to join us this evening.'

'Ah now that wouldn't be fair.'

'We're just having mince and carrots. It's no bother to set a place for an extra one.' Mr Maguire hesitated. He looked at Mary who was staring into her cup. She raised her eyes to him.

'Why don't you stay?' she said.

'Only on one condition. You must charge me extra.'

'That's settled then,' said Kathleen. 'We can haggle about the price later.'

'It's very kind of you. Both of you.'

Mr Maguire appeared at dinner time wearing a tie but no jacket. Mary sat opposite him, the tails of hair at her neck still damp from the shower, while Kathleen served and talked.

'There's a whist drive tonight in the hall, Mr Maguire. Guests are very welcome.'

'I'm sorry,' said Mr Maguire, 'I was never any good at card games — especially whist. Partners depending on you to play the right card. I played once or twice and at the finish up my shins were black and blue.'

'I *have* to go,' said Kathleen. 'I'm organizing a table.

Mary, will you run me up? I have all those cups and saucers and things.' Mary nodded.

'Can you not drive?'

'No, I'm too nervous. But Mary is very good, runs me everywhere.'

Kathleen took on the responsibility of the silences and when one occurred she talked, mostly to Mr Maguire.

'What do you do?'

'At the moment, nothing. I've just been made redundant. One of the three million.'

'Oh that's too bad.'

'Yes, when I got my redundancy money I said to heck, I'll treat myself to a holiday.'

'You were just right,' said Kathleen. 'You can't take it with you.'

'There'll be none of it left to take with me.'

Both sisters smiled. Mr Maguire looked at Mary and she felt obliged to speak.

'What did you work at?'

'In a big warehouse. Spare parts for cars.'

'Oh I see,' said Mary.

'I'd been there for most of my life.'

'Then you know a bit about cars?'

'A bit.'

'It's just that mine is not going properly.'

'What is it?'

'A Fiat.'

'No, I mean what is the problem?'

'It seems to have no power, sluggish.'

'I could have a look at it tomorrow.'

Kathleen interrupted. 'But I thought you were going tomorrow?'

'Would you mind if I stayed the weekend? I have no real reason to rush back.'

'Certainly,' said Kathleen. 'Especially if you can fix the car.'

'Thank you.' Mr Maguire had cleared his plate in a matter of minutes. Kathleen offered him second helpings.

'It's the sea air,' he said. 'Gives you an appetite. This is what I cook mostly for myself because it's easy.' Then he seemed embarrassed. 'I'm sorry. This tastes a hundred times better than my efforts. I just mean that it doesn't take much looking after on the stove.'

'I gather you don't like cooking?'

'No. At home I do a standard menu. The boiled egg. The mince. When you're on your own food doesn't seem as interesting. I find it hard enough to get through a whole loaf without it going bluemould.' He laughed. 'I eat watching the news with my plate on my knees. Rarely set a table.'

'Is there any chance you'll get another job?'

'I doubt it. The car trade is in a bad way and it's the only one I know. I'm fifty-six now. Prospects – poor.' He shrugged. Mary looked at his hands. They were big and red, making toys of his knife and fork. The nail of his thumb was opaque like a hazelnut.

'I don't really want a job,' he said. 'Now I'll have time to do what I want.'

'What's that?'

'Read. Dig my plot. I'm going to do this Open University thing. On television. I've just enrolled but it doesn't start until next January. I paid the fees out of my redundancy.'

'You make the dole sound like a good thing.'

'I've always been keen. If there's a WEA class on the go, I'm your man. History, English, Philosophy – there was a Botany year but I couldn't make head nor tail of it. Anything and everything, I'm a dabbler.'

Kathleen got out of the car at the church hall balancing a cardboard box full of trembling cups. She slammed the door with her heel.

'Hey, just you be careful with that Mr Maguire, Mary,' she said through the driver's window.

'He's a bit down-market for me, dear.' Mary laughed. 'Besides it's you he fancies.'

'Will you pick me up?'

Mary nodded.

On her way back she was irritated again by the lack of energy in the engine. On the hill of the High Street it seemed barely to have sufficient power to pull her up. She thought about Mr Maguire.

'Thank God it's Friday,' she said aloud.

77

She had kicked off her shoes and was just sitting down to look at the paper when there was a quiet rap on the door. Mr Maguire stood there with a light bulb in his hand.

'I'm sorry to trouble you,' he said, 'but my reading light has gone and I wondered if you had a spare one?' Mary, in stockinged feet, climbed on to a stool and produced a new sixty watt bulb from a high cupboard. She exchanged bulbs with him and for some reason felt foolish. He stood for a moment with the cardboard package in his hands.

'Is it raining?' he asked.

'No, not now.'

He moved the piece of card that held the bulb in place against the corrugations of the package, rippling it.

'Are you busy this evening?' he asked. Mary hesitated.

'No.'

'Would you like to go somewhere – for a drink perhaps?'

'I don't like going into pubs.'

'The hotel – we could go to the Royal, just for a while. An orange juice, if you like.'

Mary was now swinging the dead bulb by its tiny pins between her finger and thumb. 'It's Friday,' she said. 'Why not?'

Mr Maguire smiled. 'In about half an hour then?'

'Yes.'

He turned quickly, holding up the new light bulb in a gesture of thanks. For a ridiculous moment she expected it to light as if he was some kind of statue.

She closed the door and, out of habit, before she threw the used bulb in the waste-paper basket she shook it close to her ear. There was no tinkling sound. She switched off the standard lamp and removed the hot bulb with a serviette. Mr Maguire's bulb lit when she switched it on.

In the hotel lounge after the first sip of her sherry she took a tissue from her handbag and wiped the red crescent stain of her lower lip from the rim of the glass. Mr Maguire was drinking Guinness. She sat on the edge of her seat, her shoulders back. Her mother had always chivvied her about 'bearing'. One day as they walked to church she had prodded Mary between the shoulder-blades with the point of her umbrella.

'If you want to keep your bosoms separate — don't slouch.'

She could feel the ferrule to this very day. And yet now, without being told, she did everything her mother had asked of her.

'Relax,' said Mr Maguire. Muzak took away from the early evening hush.

'I'm not used to places like this. I've only been here at weddings.'

'It's a nice place.'

'The word'll be out on Monday that Miss Bradley was seen boozing with a man.'

Mr Maguire laughed.

'What do you teach?'

'German and a little French.'

'Have you been to Germany?'

'No, but I taught for a year in a German-speaking part of Switzerland. In a beautiful place called Kandersteg.'

'I've never been abroad. Never in anything bigger than a rowing-boat. And if you ever hear of me being killed in a plane crash you'll know it fell on me.'

'It was up in the mountains. A typical Swiss village with cuckoo-clock houses and snow when you looked up. The children were so well behaved it was a dream to teach there.'

Mr Maguire took out his pipe and lit it. By his face and the tilt of his head he was still listening to her.

'It was like a holiday really — it's funny how you remember the good things so vividly.'

'Maybe it's because there's so few of them,' he said. 'I remember my honeymoon as if it was yesterday. This town, your house. It was a cold summer. I sat with you by the Rayburn and we talked to the wee small hours.

'We did?'

'Well, once, maybe twice. And then one night I remember you were going to a dance. You were in your stockinged feet frantically looking for your shoes. You left a wake of scent behind you.' Mary laughed, covering her mouth with her hand. Mr Maguire drew large rings around himself with his arms. 'You were out to here with petticoats. The dress was white with green flecks in it.'

'That's right, that's right. I remember that one. Parsley

Sauce we used to call it. Those were the days when you had so few dresses you gave them names.' She rolled her eyes to heaven. It was as if he had produced an old photograph of her. 'Isn't it awful that I remember the dress but I've no recollection whatsoever of you.' Suddenly her face straightened in mock disapproval. 'And you noticed all this on your honeymoon?'

'You have no control over what you notice.'

'And where was your wife when you were sitting talking to me — to the wee small hours?'

'She was ill even then. She always went to bed early. I'm a night-owl myself.'

'Oh dear me,' she said. 'What a thing to remember — old Parsley Sauce.' Mr Maguire bought more drinks and Mary began to feel relaxed and warm.

'I'm glad we're here,' she said. 'This is nice.'

Some ex-pupils of hers came in and sat at the bar. They nodded and smirked towards the corner where she sat.

Mr Maguire asked her about what books she read and she told him she was an escapist reader. Four or five library books a week she got through. Anything, just so long as it didn't make too many demands on her. And of course nothing which would disturb. None of that embarrassing nonsense. It was hard to avoid nowadays. Library books should have warnings on the covers — be graded like films. Kathleen was different — she went in for the more heavy-weight stuff.

Mr Maguire said that unless a book was making him puzzle and think he would throw it away. He had read more first chapters than anybody else in the world. With regard to the embarrassing stuff, if it was not written for pornographic reasons he could accept it. It was a part of life the same as any other.

Mary refused another sherry saying that her head was already light, but insisted on buying Mr Maguire another bottle of Guinness, provided he wanted a third. After all, he was on the dole and she was working. When she returned with the poured glass Mr Maguire said, 'Books should not be a means of escape.'

'Why not? We're surrounded by depressing things. Who wants to read about them? When I read I prefer to be transported.' Suddenly she put her hand over her mouth in horror. 'Kathleen!' she said. 'I promised to pick up Kathleen. What time is it?'

All the lights were out in the church hall and Kathleen was pacing up and down. Mr Maguire carried her box of cups for her as Mary apologized for being late. For once Kathleen was quiet. The only sound coming from the back seat was the whine of her inhaler. In the house she slammed doors.

'There are some left-over sandwiches there,' she said.

As Mary made the tea she dropped a spoon twice and giggled. She felt very silly and likable but was aware of herself hurrying to get back to the other room where Kathleen and Mr Maguire were alone.

The next morning she slept late and was wakened by the constant revving of an engine. She looked out and saw Mr Maguire in a navy boiler suit beneath the open bonnet of her car, tinkering. Before going downstairs in her dressing-gown she freshened up and made herself look presentable. Mr Maguire came in, his oily hands aloft, and washed at the kitchen sink. Kathleen, also in her dressing-gown, offered him a cup of tea from the pot.

'I think you should see a big improvement,' he said. 'When did you last have it serviced?'

'Goodness,' said Mary. 'I can't really remember.'

'I reset your points, put in three new plugs . . . '

'I know nothing about it. You might as well be talking Double Dutch.' Mr Maguire shook his head in disbelief and sat down at the table.

'You look very smart,' said Kathleen, looking at his boiler suit.

'I always carry this in the boot. I've been caught before, changing a wheel on a wet night.'

'But it's so clean.'

Mr Maguire nodded and turned to Mary.

'Would you like to try her out?'

'Let me get dressed first. Kathleen, would you like to come for a run?'

'No, I've things to do.' She said it with an echo of the previous night's bitterness still in her voice.

'Very well, suit yourself.'

They drove towards Spanish Point. Mary was delighted with the change in the car — it even sounded different. She said so to Mr Maguire, now back in his casual wear. She herself wore trousers — a thing she never did on teaching days. Mr Maguire said, 'The thing that really fascinated me about this wreck was a ring they found. Gold, with an inscription round the inside. *No tengo mas que dar te.*' With his Belfast accent his attempt at pronunciation was comical.

Mary smiled. 'More Double Dutch.'

'It's Spanish. It means, "I have nothing more to give thee".'

'That's nice.' She changed down through the gears as they came up behind a tractor.

'I thought it very moving — to see it after all those years. What I wondered was this. Was he taking it back as a present for a loved one in Spain or had somebody given it to *him* as he sailed away with the Armada? It makes a big difference.'

'Yes, I suppose it does.' Mary indicated and passed the tractor, giving a little wave over her shoulder.

'That's Jim McLelland,' she said.

They walked awkwardly on a beach of apple-sized stones, hearing them clunk hollowly beneath their feet. Mary had to extend her arms for balance and once or twice almost had to clutch at Mr Maguire.

'This is silly,' she said. They halted and looked across at Spanish Point. Now that the rumble of stones had stopped it was very quiet.

'Mary.' Hearing him use her name for the first time she looked up startled.

'Yes?'

'You're a remarkable woman,' he said. 'I told you that I came on holiday to see this place.' He nodded to the black rocks jutting out into the sea. 'That's not the whole truth.' Mary began to feel frightened, alone on a beach with this man she hardly knew. She picked up a stone and moved it from hand to hand. It was the tone of his voice that scared her. He was weighing his words, not looking at her.

'I had a memory of this town that was sacred in a way. And over the last couple of days I realize that it is partly your fault — I don't mean fault. I mean you're part of what's good about it.' Still he didn't look at her but continued to stare out to sea. Mary could think of nothing, afraid of what he would say next.

'I had forgotten about you, but not completely. Can you imagine how surprised I was when you were still here?'

'I've no idea.' She couldn't prevent the sarcasm in her voice. But he seemed not to notice. She threw the stone with a clatter at her feet and rubbed her hands together to clean them.

'I think we'd better be getting back,' she said. They turned and began to walk towards the car.

'I'm sorry. I hope I haven't overstepped the mark.'

'I'm not sure what you mean.'

'These past few days have been very real for me. You turn out to be . . . ' he paused, 'better than I remembered. You have a kind of calm which I envy. A stillness inside.' Mary smiled at him and walked round to the driver's door.

'You don't know me at all', she said, 'if you think I'm calm and still. I'm shaking like a leaf with the kind of things you're saying.'

'I'll just say one more — and that'll be the end of it. I'd like you to think about the idea of marrying me.'

She turned to him, her eyes wide and her mouth dropping open. She laughed. 'Are you serious?'

Mr Maguire smiled slightly as he stared at her, his brow creased with wrinkles. 'Yes, I am.'

'I don't even know your first name.'

'Anthony.'

'You don't look like an Anthony, if you don't mind me saying so.'

'You don't have to say anything. All I want you to do is give it some thought.'

Mary turned on the engine, indicated left and did a U-turn to the right but stalled midway. She tried to switch on the engine again.

'What have you done to this machine?' she said.

'Would you like me to drive?'

83

Mary agreed and he drove her home in the most embarrassing silence she had ever known.

Mr Maguire climbed the stairs. Mary went straight to the kitchen where she heard Kathleen singing.

'Well?' said Kathleen. 'Big improvement?'

Mary sat down on the stool by the Rayburn. She said, 'Make me a cup of tea. I need it badly.'

'What's wrong? Did it break down?'

Mary began to laugh. 'You'll never believe this.' Her sister turned from filling the kettle. 'But I've just been proposed to.'

'What? Who?' Her voice was a screech. Mary hushed her and rolled her eyes to the ceiling as Mr Maguire closed a door. 'I don't believe you. You'll find out then if it's a real toupee.'

'It's not funny,' said Mary, still laughing. 'I was there.'

'What did you tell him?'

'I said I'd think about it.'

As Kathleen made the tea her shoulders shook.

'You'd end up keeping the shine on his wee shoes. And the crease in his boiler suit. Mother would be pleased.' She wiped her eyes and gave her sister a cup.

'You're not seriously thinking about it?'

'No, but . . . '

'But what?'

'It's just that I've never really been asked.'

'You have so. Twice. You told me.'

'But they were ludicrous.'

'And this one isn't?'

'There's something gentlemanly about him.'

'A gentleman of leisure. He's on the dole, Mary.' Kathleen grinned again. 'Did he go down on one knee?'

'Don't be silly.'

Later that afternoon when the laughter had worn off and Mr Maguire had gone for a walk Kathleen said, 'And what would become of me?'

'For goodness' sake Kathleen, I only said I would consider it.'

'I don't think I'll be able to manage on my own. Financially.'

'Kathleen! Will you excuse me. I'd like to make up my own mind on this one.'

Mary went to her bedroom and sat looking at herself in the dressing-table mirror. A hot flush came over her and she watched her face redden, like an adolescent blushing. She flinched at the thought of a kiss from Mr Maguire. And yet he would make a good companion. Eccentric, yes – but basically a good man. In so far as she knew him. Pinpoints of sweat gleamed on her forehead and upper lip. She pulled a tissue from the box on the dressing-table and dabbed herself dry, then she lay down on the bed. Perhaps she should stall him. Write letters for a period. That way things would not be complicated by his physical presence. By that time, with any luck, these fits would have passed and she would have returned to normality. Stall him. That was the answer. He would enjoy writing to her. It would give him a chance to quote poetry. For some reason Kandersteg came into her mind and with a little thrill she thought of going there on her honeymoon. In July just as soon as the school holidays had started. She would have to do all the translation for Mr Maguire. They could call and see if Herr Hauptmann was still alive and they could relive their days at the school while poor Mr Maguire would have to stare out the window at the beautiful view: the grey clouds of mist that moved against the almost black of the forest; the cleanness, the tidiness of their streets; the precision with which the trains came and went, not to the minute, but to the second; Herr Hauptmann's hazel-coloured eyes as he listened to her.

At dinner Kathleen, activated by nervousness, talked non-stop until she left the room to make the coffee. Mr Maguire nodded his head as if it had become a reflex to the torrent of words and one that he could not stop even when she had left the room. He whispered to Mary, 'Kathleen's problem is that she hasn't heard of the paragraph.' He said that he would like to settle his bill as he would be leaving first thing after Mass in the morning when the roads would be relatively traffic free.

Mary said, 'It might be nice if we walked up to the hotel later. I'd like to make my position clear.'

'Yes, that would help.'

'About eight?'

After Mr Maguire had excused himself Mary said to her sister, 'I'm going for a walk with him later.'

'It makes no difference to me. I have to go to the church to do the flowers.'

'Oh that's right. It's Saturday . . . ' Kathleen began to stack the cups on to the tray with a snatching movement.

'Have you made up your mind how you're going to tell him?'

'I'm not sure,' said Mary. 'I'm not even sure *what* I'm going to tell him.'

'Don't allow me to influence you one way or the other. You can do whatever you like. All I hope is that you won't do something you'll regret for the rest of your life. And if you go traipsing off with him I'll need some help with the mortgage.'

'There's no question of that.' Mary was aware that her voice had risen. 'You can be sure that I'll be sensible about it. If I've waited this long . . . ' Kathleen carried the tray out to the kitchen and set it on the draining-board with a crash.

At eight o'clock they both left their rooms. Mr Maguire, his shoes burnished, wearing a tie and jacket, walked like the Duke of Edinburgh, one hand holding the other by the wrist behind his back. The night was windless and at intervals between the glare of the street lights they could see stars. Mary was conscious of her heels clicking on the paving stones and was relieved when she came to the softer tarmac footpath where she could walk with more dignity.

Mr Maguire cleared his throat and asked, 'Well, did you think about what . . . ?'

'Yes, but don't talk about it now. Talk about something else.' Mr Maguire nodded in agreement and looked up at the sky for inspiration.

'What is it that makes your life worthwhile?'

'I don't know.' She laughed nervously and tried to give an answer. 'What a strange question. I suppose I help children to learn something – the rudiments of another language. And I help Kathleen who cannot work . . . '

'I don't mean worthwhile to others. But to yourself.'

'Sometimes, Mr Maguire, you say the oddest things. I'm sorry, I don't see the difference.'

'Take it from another angle. What makes you really angry?'

She felt her shoulder brush against his as they walked. 'The kind of thing that's been going on in this country. Killings, bombings . . . '

'If you were to give one good reason to stop someone blowing your head off tonight, what would it be?'

'I've jotters to correct for Monday.' Mr Maguire laughed. 'Well there's that and children and love and Kathleen . . . '

'And?'

'And I've dresses I've only worn once or twice. And the sea. And the occasional laugh in the staffroom. Just everything.'

'You would be part of the reason I would give.'

There was a long pause and Mary said, 'Thank you. That's very nice of you. But as I say I'd prefer to wait until we were settled inside before we have our little talk.' Mr Maguire shrugged and smiled. Mary veered off to look in Madge's Fashions which was still lit up. There was a single old-fashioned window model with painted brown hair instead of a wig. White flakes showed where the paint had chipped, particularly at the red fingernails.

'They've changed this dress since yesterday,' said Mary. 'I like that one better.' She joined Mr Maguire in the middle of the pavement still looking back over her shoulder.

They sat at the same table as the prevous night and Mr Maguire bought the same drinks.

'They'll be calling me a regular next,' said Mary, as he slipped into the seat beside her. 'Well now. I think . . . First of all let me say that I find it extremely difficult to talk in a situation like this. I'm out of my depth.' She tried not to sound like she was introducing a lesson, but what she said was full of considered pauses. She spoke as quietly as she could, yet distinctly. 'You are an interesting man, good — as far as I know you — but these are not reasons', she paused yet again, 'for anybody to get married. It has happened so quickly that there is an element of foolishness in it. And that's not me.'

'It's me,' said Mr Maguire, laughing.

'There are so many things. I'm not a free agent. Kathleen has got to be considered.'

'She can fairly talk.'

'Yes, sometimes it's like living with the radio on. She never expects an answer.'

'Do you love her?'

'I suppose I must. When you live with someone day in, day out, the trivial things become the most important.' She sipped her sherry and felt the glass tremble between her fingertips. 'And there are other things which frighten me. I don't think I'm that sort of person.' Mr Maguire looked at her but she was unable to hold his eye and her gaze returned to her sherry glass.

'My wife was in poor health for many, many years – so that aspect of it should not worry you. I am in the habit of – not. I would respect your wishes. Although I miss someone at my back now when I fall asleep.' Mary thought of herself slippery with sweat lying awake making sure to keep space between herself and Mr Maguire's slow breathing body.

'I can't believe this is happening to me.' She laughed and turned to face him, her hands joined firmly in her lap. 'My answer is – in the kindest possible way – no. But why don't you write to me? Why don't you come and stay with us for longer next year? Writing would be a way of getting to know each other?'

'Your answer is no – for now?'

'Yes,' said Mary. 'I mean it's ridiculous at our age.'

'I don't see why. Could I come at Christmas?'

She thought of herself and Kathleen in new dresses, full of turkey and sprouts and mince pies, dozing in armchairs and watching television for most of the day. The Christmas programmes were always the best of the year.

'No. Not Christmas.'

'Easter then?'

'Write to me and we'll see.'

Mr Maguire smiled and shrugged as if he had lost a bet.

'You've kind of taken the wind out of my sails,' he said.

The next morning when she got up Mr Maguire had gone. Kathleen had called him early and given him his breakfast.

When he had paid his bill she had deducted a fair amount for the servicing of the car.

After Mass, surrounded by the reality of the Sunday papers, Mary thought how silly the whole thing had been. The more she thought about the encounter the more distasteful it became. She resolved to answer his first letter out of politeness but, she said firmly to herself, that would be the finish of it.

On Monday she was feeling down and allowed herself the luxury of a lesson, taught to four different levels throughout the day, in which she talked about Kandersteg, its cuckoo-clock houses and the good Herr Hauptmann.

The Great Profundo

The river was so full after the recent rains that the uprights of
the bridge became like prows and for a time I was under the
impression that the bridge, with myself on it, was moving
rapidly forward. So absorbed was I in this illusion that I
accepted the sound as part of it. It was high pitched and
sentimental, sometimes submerged beneath the noise of the
traffic, sometimes rising above it, full of quaverings and
glissandi. My curiosity was aroused to see what instrument
could make such a noise. Others must have been similarly
drawn because a crowd of about fifty or sixty people had
gathered in a ring on the left bank of the river – women
shoppers, men with children on their shoulders, young fellows
elbowing each other for a better position. In the centre stood a
tall man speaking loudly and waving his arms. I edged forward
and was forced to stand on tiptoe. Still I could not trace the
source of the music which at that moment suddenly stopped.
Now everyone's attention was directed at the man in the centre
whose eyes blazed as he shouted. He walked the cobblestones
on bare feet, spinning on his heel now and again to take in the
whole circle of the crowd. On the ground in front of him was a
long, black case. With a flourish he undid the latches and flung
open the lid. Inside was red plush but I could see little else
from my position at the back.

'It is not for nothing that I am called the Great Profundo,'
shouted the man. He wore a scarlet shirt, with the sleeves

rolled up and the neck open, but his trousers looked shabby above his bare ankles. They bulged at the knees and were banded with permanent wrinkles at his groin. His hair was long and grey, shoulder length, but the front of his head was bald so that his face seemed elongated, the shape of an egg. He was not a well-looking man.

'What you will see here today may not amaze you, but I'll lay a shilling to a pound that none of you will do it. All I ask is your undivided attention.'

I noticed a figure sitting by the balustrade of the river who seemed to be taking no interest in the proceedings. He must have been the source of the earlier music because in his hand he had a violinist's bow and, between his knees, a saw. The handle rested on the ground and the teeth of the saw pointed at his chest. He was muttering to himself as he began to pack these implements into a large holdall.

'I want you to look closely at what I am about to show you.' The Great Profundo stooped to his case and produced three swords. Épées. Rubbing together their metal cup hand-guards made a distinctive hollow shearing sound. He threw one to be passed around the crowd while he clashed and scissored the other two for everyone to hear.

'Test it, ladies and gentlemen. Check that it's not like one of these daggers they use on stage. The ones where the blade slips up into the handle. There are no tricks here, citizens; what you are about to see is genuine. Genuine bedouin.'

After much to-do he swallowed the three épées (they were thin with buttons at their ends no bigger than match-heads) and staggered around the ring, his arms akimbo, the three silvery cups protruding from his mouth. The audience was impressed. They applauded loudly and goaded him on to do something even more daring.

Next he produced what looked like a cheap imitation of a sword — the kind of thing a film extra, well away from the camera, would carry. It had a broad flat aluminium blade and a cruciform handle of some cheap brassy metal. He produced a twin for it and handed them both around the crowd while he cavorted on the cobblestones shouting interminably about his lack of trickery and the genuineness of what he was about to perform.

'While I want your undivided attention, I would like you all to keep an eye out for the Law. They do not approve. They'll turn a blind eye to trumpet players, tumblers and card-sharpers, but when it comes to the idea of a man putting himself into mortal danger on the public highway they have a very different attitude.'

The crowd immediately turned their heads and looked up and down the river-bank.

'You're okay,' shouted a woman.

'On you go.'

He took back both the swords from the crowd and held them to his chest. He straddled his legs, balancing himself, and put his egg-shaped head back, opening his mouth with an elaborate and painful slowness. I felt like saying, 'Get on with it. Skip the palaver.' The man swallowed both the swords, walked around the ring, staring skywards, then hand over hand extracted them to the applause of the crowd.

'And NOW, ladies and gentlemen,' the man shouted in a voice that heralded the finale of his act, glancing over his shoulder to check that the Law, as he called them, were not to be seen, 'I will perform something which will be beyond your imagination.'

He reached into his black case and produced a sword – a long and heavy Claymore. He tried to flex it, putting all his weight on it with the sole of his bare foot, but was unable to; then with a mighty two-handed sweep he swung it at the cobblestones. It rang and sparks flew. He balanced it on its point. The blade alone reached to his receding hairline. He stood there letting the crowd take in the length of the sword he was about to swallow. He spread his arms. The spectators became silent and the noise of the traffic on the bridge was audible. He lifted it with feigned effort, balanced the blade for a moment on his chin, then lowered it hand over hand down his throat. To the hilt. When it was fully inserted the crowd cheered. Planting his bare feet, like someone in a dream, his head at right-angles to his body, I could hear even from my position at the back the harsh rasps of the performer's breath escaping past the obstruction in his throat as he moved round the ring of people.

This time I was impressed. There was no physical way he

could have swallowed that last sword – it would have had to come out of his toes. There was a trick somewhere but I joined in the applause as he withdrew the six-foot sword from his throat. At this point I felt someone push me, and the small man whom I had seen pack away his saw elbowed his way into the middle and extended his hat to begin collecting. My money was in one of my inner pockets and it would have meant unbuttoning my overcoat.

'No change,' I said.

'It's not change we want,' said the saw-player and forced his way past me. As the crowd dispersed I hung around. The Great Profundo was packing his equipment into his case. After each item he would sweep back his long hair and straighten up. The saw-player was raking through the hat, taking out the coins of the highest denomination and arranging them into columns on the balustrade. The Great Profundo sat down to put on his boots.

'Excuse me, gentlemen,' I said, dropping some coins into the hat. 'I am a student at the University and I couldn't help seeing your act. Very interesting indeed.'

'Thank you,' said Profundo. After all the shouting his voice sounded soft. 'It's nice to get praise from a man with certificates.'

'Not yet, not yet. I'm still an undergraduate. I tell you I'm a student, not for any particular reason, but because I want to make a proposition to you.' The Great Profundo looked up from his lace tying. I noticed he did not wear socks. 'I am the treasurer of a society in the University which, once or twice a year, uses live entertainment. Would either, or both, of you gentlemen be interested in performing for us?'

'How much?' asked the saw-player from the balustrade.

'We can afford only a small fee. But you may take up a collection at the actual function.'

'If they gave as much as you did just now, there'd be no point,' said the man counting the money.

'What would the University want to look at the likes of us for?' the Great Profundo said, smiling at the thought.

'Our society certainly would. It's called the "Eccentrics Genuine Club". We meet every month and have a few pints, sometimes entertainment.'

This was not the whole truth. We had met twice that year, and on both occasions the entertainment had been female strippers.

'Who?' asked the saw-player.

'Musicians. The occasional singer. That kind of thing.'

'We'll think about it,' said the Great Profundo. He wrote out his address and I said I would contact him after the next committee meeting.

As I walked away from them I heard the saw-player say, 'Eight pounds, some odds.'

'If my mother was alive, Jimmy, she'd be proud of me. Going to the University.' The Great Profundo laughed and stamped his boot on the ground.

The committee of the Eccentrics Genuine Club was delighted with the idea and even suggested a more generous sum of money than they had given to each of the strippers. However, divided between two entertainers, it still wasn't enough. I made a speech in which I said that if they valued their reputation for eccentricity – haw-haw – they would fork out a little more. A saw-player and a sword-swallower on University territory! What a coup! Who could refuse, no matter what the cost? The committee eventually approved, somewhat reluctantly, twice the sum given to the strippers. And they had no objection to a collection being taken on the night of the performance.

With this news and the idea of interviewing him for the University newspaper, I drove to the Great Profundo's. It was a part of the city where walls were daubed with slogans and topped with broken glass. I parked and locked the car. Then, seeing some children playing on a burst sofa on the pavement, I checked each door-handle and took my tape-recorder with me. It was an expensive one – the type professional broadcasters use – which my father had bought me when I'd expressed an interest in journalism.

There was a selection of names on bits of paper beneath the doorbells of the tenement. The name on the bell of 14c was Frankie Taylor. I rang it and waited. Papers and dust swirled in the corners. A window opened and the man himself leaned out.

94

'Remember me?' I shouted. The figure at the window nodded and waved me up. The stone stairway smelled badly of cooked food. The Great Profundo was on the landing, waiting barefoot, when I reached the fourth floor.

'Yes, I remember,' he said and shook hands. 'The student. Those stairs knacker the best of us.' He led me, breathing heavily, into the flat and offered me a chair which I declined. Would he be free – would he and the saw-player be free – on the evening of the thirteenth of next month? The sword-swallower shrugged and said that it was very likely. He sat down in his armchair and folded his knees up to his chest. Then he sprang up again and asked me if I would like a cup of coffee. I refused politely. I offered to write down the date and time of the meeting but Profundo assured me that they would be there. He sat down again and began to finger his toes.

'Would you like a beer?'

'What kind?'

He jumped off the chair and said, 'I'll see what I've left. I didn't know you'd be coming.' He opened a cupboard and closed it again, then left the room. I went over to the window to check that my car was still in one piece.

Profundo came back with three cans of lager held together by plastic loops.

'Tennent's. From Christmas,' he said. He jerked one free and handed it over and took another himself. 'Don't be worrying about the car. It's safe enough down there. The neighbours will keep an eye on it.'

I took the seat he had previously offered and said, 'There's another thing I'd wanted to ask you. I work for a student newspaper, *Rostrum*, and I was wondering how you would feel about giving an interview some time.'

'Me?' I applied pressure to the ring-pull and the can snapped open. From the triangular hole the lager was fizzy and tepid. 'Why me? What could I tell you?'

'Our readers are interested in a lot of things. I'm sure with the life you've led it couldn't fail.'

'Aww here now . . . ' He laughed and looked down at his feet. Without Jimmy, the saw-player, he seemed defenceless. He was a shy man, unable to look me in the eye. His voice

95

was quiet, conversational – not strident like he had been by the river-bank.

'If it's of any help to you . . . in your studies, like . . . Oh would you like a glass?'

'No thanks,' I said. 'Are you busy? Would you mind doing it now?'

'Do I look busy?' he said spreading his hands. I set up my machine, took a slug from the can and began my interview. (*See Appendix.*)

The bar in the students' Union was hired for the night of the thirteenth and a low platform stage erected against one wall. In my role as treasurer I was obliged to be around so another of the members of the Eccentrics Genuine was sent in his car to pick up the pair of performers. There was a splendid turn-out – everyone in formal evening wear – and I was pleased at the thought of covering expenses from the door money alone. After that, what we made on new membership and the bar was profit. I myself was responsible for about forty new members that night: part of the rugby club, friends from the Young Conservatives, Engineers, Medics and, most extraordinary of all, some people from a recently formed Society of Train-spotters.

The entertainment was due to begin at nine o'clock and for about an hour and a half before that the bar was pandemonium. I have never seen students drink so much – even the Eccentrics Genuine. As early as eight o'clock they all began clapping and singing 'Why are we waiting?' But it was all very good-humoured.

At a quarter to nine I was informed of the arrival of the artists and went to welcome them. They were both standing in the corridor outside. The Great Profundo shook hands warmly. Jimmy nodded and said to me, 'Is there anywhere we can change, get the gear sorted?'

'Pardon?'

'Like a dressing-room?'

'No. No I'm sorry. I hadn't thought you would need one – what with the street and all that.'

'Street is street and indoors is indoors.'

'It's okay, this'll do,' said Profundo. He began stripping off his checked shirt and getting into his scarlet one. He had a surprisingly hairy chest. 'You go ahead, Jimmy, warm them up.' Jimmy continued grumbling and got out his bow and saw. Profundo edged past him and took a look through the glass doors.

'A full house, by the look of it.' Then he stopped. 'Is there no women in there?'

'Not in the Eccentrics Genuine,' I said. 'It's one of the Club rules.'

'We're not *that* eccentric,' said another member of the Committee. 'We know how to enjoy ourselves.'

I slipped in at the back to listen to Jimmy's performance. The melody he played was the same one I had heard that day on the bridge but within the confines of the hall it sounded different, more sentimental. The notes soared and trembled and swooped. One member of the audience, just to my left, took out a white handkerchief and pretended to mop his eyes. In playing the saw there is a great deal of vibrato required to give the notes texture. The player's left hand quivers as the saw changes pitch.

'He's got Parkinson's disease,' shouted one of the new Medic members. But apart from that he was listened to attentively and applauded when he finished his selection.

Afterwards there was a great dash for the bar. Everyone considered it an interval and I had to hold back the Great Profundo until the crowd was settled again, which took some considerable time. While he waited patiently I pointed out to him that the floor was awash with beer, which might be awkward for him in his bare feet.

'And now, gentlemen of the Eccentrics Genuine Club, it is my great pleasure to introduce to you the one and only, the great, the profound, the Great Profundo . . . ' I gave him such a buildup in the old music-hall manner that the audience were on their feet applauding as he made his entrance. He ran, carrying his black case on his shoulders, and took a jump up on to the stage. For a man of his age he was almost lithe. His movements as he opened his box of tricks were sweeping and athletic.

On my first encounter with him I had not noticed that his

patter, which he began almost immediately he reached the stage, was so juvenile. He had not tailored his talk for such an audience as the Eccentrics Genuine. They laughed politely at some of his jokes. When he inserted the three épées and held his arms out wide for approval there was a kind of ironic cheer. His act lacked music and somebody began a drum-roll on one of the tables. This was taken up throughout the room until the bar throbbed with noise. Some others began to imitate a fanfare of trumpets. When he inserted the two aluminium film-extra swords someone said, not loudly, but loudly enough, 'He's naive. He'd swallow anything.' There was a great deal of laughter at this, suppressed at first in snorts and shoulder-shaking, but which finally burst out and echoed round the bar. He silenced them by taking out the Claymore. There was a small three-legged stool beside him, on which Jimmy had sat to play his saw, and the Great Profundo, with gritted teeth, swung the broadsword and imbedded the blade a full inch into it. He had to put his foot on the stool and tug with all his might to free it and this occasioned yet more laughter. He stood the point of the sword on the small stage to let them see the length of it in relation to his height. A voice said, 'If you stuck it up your arse we'd be impressed.'

And yet he went on. He did his hand over hand lowering of the blade into the depths of himself to the accompaniment of drumming on the tables. When it was fully inserted, he spread his arms, put his head back and paraded the stage. Some of the crowd were impressed because they cheered and clapped but others kept laughing, maybe because they were drunk, maybe at a previous joke. Then the tragedy happened.

The crowd could see it coming because they suddenly quietened. With his head back the Great Profundo took one or two paces forward and stepped off the edge of the platform. He came down heavily on his right foot which slipped on the wet floor. He managed to remain upright but uttered a kind of deep groan or retch which everyone in the audience heard. He stood there, not moving, for several seconds, then he withdrew the sword and made his exit. Some of the crowd stood and applauded, others made straight for the bar. Jimmy tussled among them with a yellow plastic bucket to take up a collection.

Afterwards in the corridor I apologized for the behaviour and handed over the cheque to the Great Profundo.

'It's both on the one. I didn't know Jimmy's second name so I made it all out to Frankie Taylor.'

'Thanks.' In the corridor lights Profundo's face looked grey.

'I'll take it,' said Jimmy. 'Your audience is a bunch of shit.'

'I think we may have opened the bar too early. I'm sorry.'

'You're right there. All the fuckin money's going over the counter. They gave three pounds. I haven't seen pennies in a bucket for twenty years.'

Before putting the Claymore back in its case Frankie wiped its blade with a small damp cloth. Against the whiteness I saw specks of red.

'Will you not have a drink?' I said. 'On the house.'

They refused. They were in a hurry to leave.

When I rang the bell of 14c it was Jimmy who put his head out of the window and called me up. The door was ajar when I reached the fourth floor. Jimmy was searching for something in a cupboard. He barely looked up at me.

'Where's the man himself?' I said.

'Did you not hear? He's in hospital.'

'What?'

'He was pishing black for a week before he went to see about it. Must have been bleeding inside.'

'Is it serious?'

'They don't know whether he'll do or not. If you saw the colour of him you wouldn't hold out much hope.'

Jimmy continued to rummage among the clothes and papers. He lifted a black brassière and looked at it.

'Where the hell did he get all the women's stuff?' he muttered, more to himself than to me. 'What did you want to see him about?'

'Just to say hello. And to tell him the article will be in the next issue.'

'A lot of good that'll do him.'

He held a pullover up to his chest, saw the holes in the sleeves and threw it back into the cupboard.

'I also wanted to return something I'd borrowed.'

'What?'

'To do with the article.'

'I'll give it to him.'

'I'd prefer to hold on to it, if you don't mind.'

'Suit yourself,' he said and closed the cupboard door. 'But the man'll be dead before the week's out.'

APPENDIX
THE GREAT PROFUNDO — SWORD-SWALLOWER
(*Rostrum* vol. 37, no. 18)

The interviewer deliberated long and hard about whether or not to include certain parts of the following material but felt justified in doing so because it is the truth. Once a writer, be he novelist, critic or journalist, fails to report the world AS HE SEES IT then he has failed in his craft.

The interviewer visited the subject at his home in Lower Coyle Street. The apartments were small and sparsely furnished with little regard for order or taste. It was a sparseness which derived not from asceticism but poverty. During the interview the subject was, at first, nervous — particularly about speaking in the presence of a tape-recorder — then, when he forgot about it, animated. Throughout the subject was barefoot and fiddled continually with his toes.

INTERVIEWER: Could you tell us something about how you became involved in such an odd profession?

PROFUNDO: Is it on now? Okay. Right. Oh God, I don't know. I was always interested in circuses and things. It was about the only entertainment we ever got where I was brought up.

INTERVIEWER: Where was that?

PROFUNDO: In the country — a village about thirty miles south of here. The circus would come through about twice a year. In the summer and maybe at Christmas. I just loved the whole thing. The smell of the animals — the laugh you had when they crapped in the ring. Some of those people! One minute you'd see them collecting money at the door, the next they'd be up on a trapeze. No safety-net, either. Anyway, I was about sixteen at the time and they'd organized a speed-drinking contest. I didn't want to win in case my mother found out — she was very wary of the drink — but I could pour a pint down like that. (*He mimics the action.*) Like down a funnel. I have no thrapple, y'see. It was a fire-eater who told me this — I thought I was just normal. He took me under his wing and got me at the sword-swallowing.

INTERVIEWER: Did you join the circus?

PROFUNDO: Not that year, but I did the next. That was the year they had the six-legged calf. It's a thing I don't like — the way they use freaks. I don't mean the wee midgets and all that — they earn good money and they can't work at much else. But I remember paying to go into a tent to see this beast. It was just deformed, that's all. Two half-bent extra legs sticking out its behind. I felt sorry for it — and a bit sick. But I said nothing. They took me on as a roustabout. I tried all kinds of things at the beginning. Acrobat — anything anybody would teach me.

(At this point the subject demonstrated a one-armed horizontal handstand on the edge of the table. The sight brought to mind the paintings of Chagall where peasants float above their world with no visible means of suspension. This physical activity seemed to banish his nervousness and he warmed to his theme.)

That's not good for me at my age. It's why I concentrate on swords now. Doesn't take as much out of you.

INTERVIEWER: Do you still enjoy it?

PROFUNDO: It's hard graft in all weathers and lately I've begun to have my doubts. But if I gave it up what could I do? How'd I pass the day? One of my main difficulties is that I'm not good with an audience. There's guys can come out and have a crowd eating out of their hand right away with a few jokes. That's hooring. All the time they're saying, 'Like me, like me for myself. It doesn't matter what my act is, I want you to like *me*.' If your act is no good, what's the point. It's the reason *you* are out there instead of one of them. People love to think they could do it — with a bit of practice. That's what's behind the oldest trick in the circus. Somebody asks for a volunteer and grabs a woman from the audience. He throws her around — on a horse or a trapeze or a trampoline — and we get flashes of her knickers, and all the time she's holding on to her handbag. You'd be amazed at how many people fall for it. But it's a plant. I loved playing that part — sitting up on the benches pretending you were the little old lady.

INTERVIEWER: And when did you begin to major in the sword-swallowing?

PROFUNDO: Oh that must have been thirty years ago. It was a good act — then. Not the way you saw it the other day. (*Laughs*) In those days I had STYLE. A rig-out like one of those bull-fighters, gold braid on scarlet, epaulettes, the long black hair and a voice that'd lift the tent. And the swords. D'you see those things I've got now? Rubbish — except for the Claymore.

INTERVIEWER: What happened to the good ones?

PROFUNDO: I'm sure they ended up in the pawn. But it wasn't me put them there. D'you know the way I hand them round for the people to test? Well there's some cities I've been in — I'll not mention their names — when I handed them round they never came back. Somebody buggered off with them. But times were very hard just after the war. I don't really blame people. You deserve all you get handing expensive items like that into a crowd. But some of them were real beauties. I collected them all over Europe.

INTERVIEWER: I didn't realize you'd been that far afield.

PROFUNDO: After the war in France was the best. People had seen such desperate things. They wanted to be amused, entertained.

INTERVIEWER: But there couldn't have been a lot of money about — just after the war.

PROFUNDO: Whose talking about money? I'm talking about when it was best to be in front of an audience. They appreciated me. I had fans. Artists came to draw me.

INTERVIEWER: Artists?

PROFUNDO: Well, one artist — but he came time and time again. I didn't know who he was at the time — a small man with a white beard and glasses. He didn't talk much — just drew all the time.

(*At this point the subject sprang from his seat and rummaged beneath his bed and produced a dog-eared folder from a suitcase. It contained newspaper clippings and photographs of himself and in a cellophane envelope a signed drawing by Matisse.*) (*See Illustration.*)

What do you think of that, eh?

INTERVIEWER: This must be worth thousands.

PROFUNDO: I know it's valuable but I wouldn't sell it. Not at

all. I didn't much like it at the beginning – I mean it's just . . .
But I got to like it the more I looked at it. He did about thirty of
me. Somebody tells me there's one hanging in New York
somewhere.

INTERVIEWER: Do you think I could borrow it to reproduce
with the article?

PROFUNDO: Sure. But I'd like to have it back.

INTERVIEWER: Of course. Why don't you frame it and put it
on the wall.

PROFUNDO: You'd just get used to it then. This way I see it
once every couple of years – when somebody calls. Then it's
fresh. Far better under the bed. The last time it was out was to
show to Jimmy. He didn't think much of it.

INTERVIEWER: I was going to ask you about him. Where does
he fit in?

PROFUNDO: I met Jimmy a couple of years ago when I came
back to work this place. The hardest thing about street work is
gathering a crowd. He does that for me. The sound of that
bloody saw attracts them from miles away and they all stand
about listening. Once they're all there I go straight into the
routine. We split the proceeds. Jimmy has a good money head
on him.

INTERVIEWER: I'd say so.

(*The subject offered his last can of lager which was refused. He went to
the kitchen to get two glasses in order to share it. In his absence the
interviewer noticed that the subject had, in his rummagings in one of the
cupboards, disturbed a box, which on closer inspection was seen to contain
a variety of ladies' underwear. The interviewer in all innocence asked the
following question when the subject returned.*)

INTERVIEWER: Do you have family? Daughters?

PROFUNDO: No? I'm by myself here.

(*The subject then realized that the question was brought about by the
contents of the box. He seemed embarrassed.*)

Oh that. You weren't meant to see those. Is that machine of
yours still going?

INTERVIEWER: No. I've switched it off now. I hope you're not
offended by this question, but are you homosexual?

PROFUNDO: No, I'm not offended and no, I'm not a homosexual. I've been in love with many women in my time. Sometimes I like to imagine myself as one. Wearing their clothes is a kind of tribute to them. It does no one any harm.

INTERVIEWER: (*After an awkward silence*) And how do you see the future?

PROFUNDO: I wait for it to come and then look at it (*laughs*).

INTERVIEWER: And lastly what about trade secrets? Can you tell any?

PROFUNDO: There aren't any to tell. You'd better switch your machine on again. Okay? Trade secrets. I used to keep the blades very clean – wipe them down with spirit. But there's as many germs on the bread that goes into your stomach, so after a while I stopped that.

INTERVIEWER: But *how* on earth do you swallow that big one?

PROFUNDO: The Claymore? The same way as all the others. It's a craft. I can't explain it. I once worked with a man who could eat light bulbs, pins and needles, but I could never do that kind of thing. My talent is different.

INTERVIEWER: Thank you.

Remote

Around about the end of each month she would write a letter, but because it was December she used an old Christmas card, which she found at the bottom of the biscuit tin among her pension books. She stood dressed in her outdoor clothes on tiptoe at the bedroom window waiting for the bird-watcher's Land Rover to come over the top of the hill two miles away. When she saw it she dashed, slamming the door after her and running in her stiff-legged fashion down the lane on to the road. Her aim was to be walking, breathing normally, when the Land Rover would indicate and stop in the middle of the one-track road.

'Can I give you a lift?'

'Aye.'

She walked round the front of the shuddering engine and climbed up to sit on the split seat. Mushroom-coloured foam bulged from its crack. More often than not she had to kick things aside to make room for her feet. It was not the lift she would have chosen but it was all there was. He shoved the wobbling stick through the gears and she had to shout — each month the same thing.

'Where are you for?'

'The far side.'

'I'm always lucky just to catch you.'

He was dressed like one of those hitch-hikers, green khaki jacket, cord trousers and laced-up mountain boots. His hair was long and unwashed and his beard divided into points like the teats of a goat.

'Are you going as far as the town this time?'

'Yes.'

'Will you drop me off?'

'Sure. Christmas shopping?'

'Aye, that'll be right.'

The road spun past, humping and squirming over peat bogs, the single track bulging at passing places – points which were marked by tall black and white posts to make them stand out against the landscape. Occasionally in the bog there were incisions, a black-brown colour, herring-boned with scars where peat had been cut.

'How's the birds doing?' she shouted.

'Fine. I've never had so many as this year.'

His accent was English and it surprised her that he had blackheads dotting his cheekbones and dirty hands.

'Twenty-two nesting pairs – so far.'

'That's nice.'

'Compared with sixteen last year.'

'What are they?'

He said what they were but she couldn't hear him properly. They joined the main road and were silent for a while. Then rounding a corner the bird-man suddenly applied the brakes. Two cars, facing in opposite directions, sat in the middle of the road, their drivers having a conversation. The bird-man muttered and steered round them, the Land Rover tilting as it mounted the verge.

'I'd like to see them try that in Birmingham.'

'Is that where you're from?'

He nodded.

'Why did you come to the island?'

'The birds.'

'Aye, I suppose there's not too many down there.'

He smiled and pointed to an open packet of Polo mints on the dashboard. She lifted them and saw that the top sweet was soiled, the relief letters almost black. She prised it out and gave it to him. The white one beneath she put in her mouth.

'Thanks,' she said.

'You born on the island?'

'City born and bred.' She snorted. 'I was lured here by a man forty-two years ago.'

'I never see him around.'

'I'm not surprised. He's dead this long time.' She cracked the ring of the mint between her teeth.

'I'm sorry.'

She chased the two crescents of mint around with her tongue.

'What did he do?'

'He drowned himself. In the loch.'

'I'm sorry, I didn't mean that.'

'On Christmas Day. He was mad in the skull — away with the fairies.'

There was a long pause in which he said again that he was sorry. Then he said, 'What I meant was — what did he do for a living?'

'What does it matter now?'

The bird-man shook his head and concentrated on the road ahead.

'He was a shepherd,' she said. Then a little later, 'He was the driver. There should always be one in the house who can drive.'

He let her off at the centre of the village and she had to walk the steep hill to the Post Office. She breathed through her mouth and took a rest halfway up, holding on to a small railing. Distances grew with age.

Inside she passed over her pension book, got her money and bought a first-class stamp. She waited until she was outside before she took the letter from her bag. She licked the stamp, stuck it on the envelope and dropped it in the letter box. Walking down the hill was easier.

She went to the Co-op to buy sugar and tea and porridge. The shop was strung with skimpy tinselled decorations and the music they were playing was Christmas hits — 'Rudolf' and 'I saw Mammy Kissing Santa Claus'. She only had a brief word with Elizabeth at the check-out because of the queue behind her. In the butcher's she bought herself a pork chop and some bacon. His bacon lasted longer than the packet stuff.

When she had her shopping finished she wondered what to do to pass the time. She could visit young Mary but if she did that she would have to talk. Not having enough things to say she felt awkward listening to the tick of the clock and the distant cries of sea birds. Chat was a thing you got out of the habit of when you were on your own all the time and, besides, Mary was shy. Instead she decided to buy a cup of tea in the café. And treat herself to an almond bun. She sat near the window where she could look out for the post van.

The café was warm and it, too, was decorated. Each time the door opened the hanging fronds of tinsel fluttered. On a tape somewhere carols were playing. Two children, sitting with their mother, were playing with a new toy car on the table-top. The cellophane wrapping had been discarded on the floor. They both imitated engine noises although only one of them was pushing it round the plates. The other sat waiting impatiently for his turn.

She looked away from them and stared into her tea. When they dredged him up on Boxing Day he had two car batteries tied to his wrists. He was nothing if not thorough. One of them had been taken from his own van parked by the loch shore and the thing had to be towed to the garage. If he had been a drinking man he could have been out getting drunk or fallen into bad company. But there was only the black depression. All that day the radio had been on to get rid of the dread.

When 'Silent Night' came on the tape and the children started to squabble over whose turn it was she did not wait to finish her tea but walked slowly to the edge of the village with her bag of shopping, now and again pausing to look over her shoulder. The scarlet of the post van caught her eye and she stood on the verge with her arm out. When she saw it was Stuart driving she smiled. He stopped the van and she ducked down to look in the window.

'Anything for me today?'

He leaned across to the basket of mail which occupied the passenger seat position and began to rummage through the bundles of letters and cards held together with elastic bands.

'This job would be all right if it wasn't for bloody Christmas.' He paused at her single letter. 'Aye, there's just one.'

'Oh good. You might as well run me up, seeing as you're going that way.'

He sighed and looked over his shoulder at a row of houses. 'Wait for me round the corner.'

She nodded and walked on ahead while he made some deliveries. The lay-by was out of sight of the houses and she set her bag down to wait. Stuart seemed to take a long time. She looked down at the loch in the growing dark. The geese were returning for the night, filling the air with their squawking. They sounded like a dance-hall full of people laughing and enjoying themselves, heard from a distance on the night wind.

Death of a Parish Priest

His niece brought him a hot whiskey and set it on the bookshelf beside him, the cloves still circulating. There was a white speckle of undissolved sugar turning in the bottom of the glass.

'Good on you, Molly,' he said. For a time he did not touch it but alternately read his book and stared into the fire, listening to Molly rattling plates and cutlery in the kitchen. When he did lift the drink he inhaled the fumes and the vaporized alcohol caught his breath.

'Are you all right?' said Molly. She was wearing her overcoat and came and sat on the edge of the armchair opposite him. His coughing stopped and he nodded and sipped the whiskey to clear his throat. 'Now keep a good fire on. I've left coal in for you because that back step is like a skating-rink.'

'Thanks.'

'And don't you even *think* about going over to that church to say your prayers tonight. The forecast is for minus twelve. Magee will see to everything.'

'What would I do without you, Molly?'

'There's more than you depending on me. I'm going home to a houseful of gulpins who claim they don't know where the kettle is.' She stood up and wrapped her woollen scarf twice round her neck. 'Good night. I'll see you in the morning.

'Good night, Molly.'

The door of the parochial house slammed and he heard the fading crackle of his niece's footsteps over the frozen ground. He went to the kitchen, to where she usually hid the bottle, poured himself another whiskey and drank it straight off without water. It burned him on its way down. He put on his collar and a jacket, picked up his stick from the hallstand and went out. Gingerly he stepped down the two steps, taking the weight on his stick. The lights were still on, shining through the stained glass rose-window. Above that the high roof was black against a sky glittering with stars in the frost.

On entering the church he knew there was something wrong. Through habit he tried to cross himself but, when dipping, his fingers struck a kind of false bottom. His middle finger stubbed too soon against marble. He looked into the font and saw that the holy water was frozen into a solid disc at the bottom.

That would keep most people at home. The prayers would have to be very urgent to bring any of the old ones out on such a night. Only two of the main lights were on, spotlighting the altar so that the sides and back of the church were in almost total darkness. He made his way over to the group of statues at the right-hand side and hooked his stick on the nearest pew. There was a cushioned chair facing the life-size group of the Crucifixion and he sat down, accepting that he was too old to kneel. His breath, even inside the church, was visible. He prayed for his niece and her family, then for the happy repose of the souls of his mother and father. His prayers had a routine about them so that no one should be forgotten. He let his head sink forward on to his chest and then woke with a start.

'Forgive me, Lord. I could not watch five minutes with you, never mind the full hour.' He repeated the prayers for his parents just in case, with the drowsiness, they had not been effective. The bakery was warmth and the sweet breath of bread from the ovens. His father had gone to bed at nine o'clock and risen at four-thirty. The old priest cupped his hands and blew into them. Sometimes his father had let him help with the knocking back of the dough. He had seen him fold it, awkward as a down mattress, press it, bang it, hammer the air out of it. When the boy tried he seemed so puny that his father would say, 'Here, let a man at it,' and he would fold the pale mass on the floured bench — half over, then the sides in like an envelope — and bang it with the heel of his hand. Bread of heaven. It had no yeast in it. Made by the nuns in Belfast. White as snow. His father had a grey complexion and his hair was gingery white. Whether or not it was from the flour the boy didn't know — he didn't think of such things and accepted him as a greyish man. The flour certainly got inside him — that was why he died so young. The wheezes in his chest were awful to listen to in the quiet of the kitchen. If they were really bad he would say, 'Excuse the bagpipes,' and give a cough that made everybody who heard it look away from him. Like stones rumbling at the bottom of an enamel pail. When he was forty-five they moved his bed downstairs because the climb at night had become an impossibility.

He had had the Crucifixion group recently repainted and it was only now when it was obliquely lit that he noticed that the artist had added varnished tears to Our Blessed Lady's cheeks. He had not been consulted but it was a nice touch. The only woman he'd ever loved. He looked at Mary Magdalen to see if tears had been added to her. Indeed they had. He gave a low whistle. If he moved his head from side to side they gleamed in the shadows.

Not true that — about the only woman. There had been Joy. Joy MacMullen. A housekeeper, fifteen years his junior, during the war. But he had never so much as laid a hand on her shoulder. He had loved her from afar. Aching to be silent and close to her. Closing his eyes, not knowing whether it was through remorse or pleasure. She was not pretty, but had eyes that spoke to him and a grace in her movements which demanded his notice. And she could take a joke. 'Come with me, under my coat, and we will drink our fill of the milk of the white goat, or wine if it be thy will.'

'You and your books,' was all she'd said. She had worked for him for a year and a half then one day went off, without so much as a by your leave, to marry a school teacher from County Fermanagh. For three Christmases she sent him a card, then he never heard from her again. Her replacement was a good woman, but withered.

It was strange how the pun fitted — kneading bread. Hunger. Soul hunger — needing Christ. The lonely sheep look up and are not fed. Was it lonely? How could the word be lonely if sheep was plural? Hungry — it must be the hungry sheep who looked up.

That was not strictly true either — not putting his hand on her shoulder. One day he had found her in tears with a telegram in her hand. Her younger brother had been killed in the war, in France. He had put his arms around her and felt her sobs. Felt her haunch against his, her chest against his, the bones of her back moving beneath his hand. They had remained so for some time, he enjoying her proximity and her smell.

His head dipped, then snapped back up again. This must be what it was like listening to a sermon. From the pulpit he could see and forgive men, still in their working clothes, their heads nodding down on to their chests. She had a mole the size of a shirt-button on the back of her neck, visible only when she wore her hair up. Her head slowly descending . . . the nape of her neck . . . white as . . . bread . . . bed linen . . .

He woke with a loud bang to find himself in total darkness — not total, he could see the red pin-prick of the sanctuary lamp at the side of the main altar. He tried to figure out what the noise had been. Had something fallen? Magee. It had been Magee closing the place up. He got to his feet and sweeping his stick to and fro in front of him like a blind man made it to the porch. He heard the sexton's distant tuneless whistle fading. He tried the door but it was locked. He banged it with his stick. The fool mustn't have seen him. Or saw him and thought he was part of the Crucifixion, dammit. Turn on the lights and perhaps he'll see them and realize something is wrong. He stumbled over a chair left in the porch for people who fainted at Mass. Eventually he found the switches and turned two on. No need for the whole lot. Magee was continually fighting him over his economies.

'It's not you who has to pay the bills at the end of the month, Magee. *C'est moi.*'

He walked up the aisle, then through the sacristy to try the sacristy door but it too was locked from the outside. Magee was efficient, if nothing else. What a pickle to be in! There was no phone. In the church he was cut off from the outside world. If the worst came to the worst he could sleep on the hassocks the altar boys knelt on at Mass. He was beginning to feel tired. But something told him that he should not sleep. He tried some of the windows but they had become so cemented over the years with accumulated coats of magnolia paint that he knew it was hopeless. Very tired. And breathless with straining. He wandered out on to the terrazzo altar, jigging his knee instead of a proper genuflection as he passed the tabernacle and stood looking down the church. He climbed to the organ loft thinking that if passers-by heard the sounds they would feel something was amiss. He switched it on and sat down on the bench. Pressing his left foot down he heard the deep throb of the droning note echo round the church. He could not play but pressed various keys on the keyboard and liked the sound of them, triplets of notes with his fingers, pedal notes with his feet. If only he could play he could while away the time. Some Bach or a little Buxtehude. He pulled out various stops to hear what difference it made to the notes. Chords. Best with the left hand. Boom. That summer he had spent near Castel Gandolfo − the heat − closing over the shutters in his room so that it *looked* cooler. From somewhere nearby, it sounded like an orphanage with its high abandoned voices, a record of Guy Mitchell played again and again and again. Chick-a-boom, chick-a-rac. Pius the Twelfth − austere, ascetic. Nothing had prepared him for meeting him in the flesh. In immaculate white. Here was a man who carried his authority with humility. All his life as a priest Tom had been wary of bishops and cardinals − the storm troopers. He had his own way of going about things. Chick-a-boom, chick-a-rac.

He looked up into the mirror on the organ and saw a figure sitting in front of the main altar, her black shawl up over her head. He turned and went down the stairs and up the middle aisle. There was something in the tilt of her shoulder, the way she sat, that made him guess who it was. He walked up the middle aisle and paused. She looked round at him.

'Mama.'

She patted the hard wood of the bench beside her. 'Sit

down, Tom,' she said. 'Are you sure you're warm enough? It's bitter cold.

'"Poor Tom's a-cold."'

'What?'

'It's a quote. From King Lear. A play, mother.'

'Oh.'

'What are you doing here?'

Her face was older than he had remembered it — small pouches, the shape of half moons, lay beneath her eyes. The left eye wept water which she dabbed away with a handkerchief bunched like a drumstick head in her hand. The lower lid hung red and angry-looking.

'And how are you?' she said.

'Fine. Molly, Bridie's girl, is looking after me now — lives just around the corner. If you'd arranged it yourself, it couldn't have worked out better.' She reached out her hand and touched his. She was colder than he was and what little heat there was in him seemed to leave him and go to her. He shuddered involuntarily, like the way he did sometimes when he'd emptied his bladder. The heat leaving him.

'I never liked to touch you,' he said, 'and you continually made me.'

'It was my condition. I thought it was wind. Rubbing my back used to relieve it. I'm sorry. If I'd known I wouldn't have asked.'

'Don't be like that. At least let us be pleasant to one another. Tell me something happy.'

She looked down at her hands and began to rotate her wedding ring. Her knuckles were red and swollen, whether with work or the cold he couldn't tell.

'The day you were ordained I was happy.' She smiled. 'It was the first time I ever tasted pineapple.' She dabbed at her eye with the handkerchief. 'And the day you were born. The days all of you were born. God rewards you with happiness for the struggle.'

'Being celibate I don't even have my Cordelia to weep over.'

'What does that mean? I don't like that word — celibate. It gives me a funny feeling. Talk about something else.'

'I have lost my teeth. I have to wear false ones. But I take them out when I'm saying Mass. Somehow I feel it is not right. Christ's Body and Blood.'

'Wrap up warm, Tom. You're beginning to look very pale.'

'And I feel sleepy.'

'Your skin is like ice. You mustn't sleep. Not now. Move about.'

'I will. You're right.'

He got up from the pew and moved on to the altar. Time was when he'd have had to open a gate. Now it was all different. The congregation had to be part of the Mass — it was even wrong to call it that. It was the Celebration of the Eucharist now. Hard to teach an old dog new tricks. God be with the days when the whole thing was in Latin and he had the privacy of his back to the people. Now he was like a master of ceremonies at a meeting in the parochial hall. He took the two hassocks for the altar-boys and laid them side by side. Mustn't sleep. He looked back over his shoulder but his mother had gone.

In the vestry he opened the wardrobe door and took down a cope encrusted with gold braid and embroidered in heavy coloured threads. Done by nuns — Dublin this time. He carried it on to the altar and found that he was exhausted by the effort. Had I the heavens' embroidered cloths, enwrought with golden and silver light . . . He sat on the first step of the altar. Then lowered himself on to the makeshift mattress. The cold radiated from the terrazzo floor. He pulled the cope up around him. It was rough and jagged against his cheek. He pushed it down a little and lay staring at the perspective of the middle aisle. Someone moved in the shadows at the back. He said who is it but the words barely came out. Then a figure appeared and walked slowly towards him. She was dressed in a white blouse and grey skirt. Her hair was up. She came to him, stepped out of her shoes and sat sideways on the strip of carpet which led up the steps to the tabernacle. He lifted his arm with a great effort and raised the side of the cope, beckoning her. She smiled and lay down beside him.

'We need do nothing. Except be close. Be warm. Be . . . Joy . . .'

Some Surrender

Two figures move slowly up the steep angle of the Hill, waist deep in gorse and bracken. The man taking up the rear, by far the younger of the two, is dressed in anorak and climbing boots while his companion wears a light sports-jacket, collar and tie and ordinary brightly polished shoes. The older man walks with his arms swinging, leaning into the slope. Strung tightly over his shoulder is the strap of a binocular case which raps and bobs against his back. There is a spring in his step and he tends to climb the narrow path on his toes. The more bulky man behind is breathing heavily and placing his hands on his thighs and pushing against them for leverage. At this point the Hill is like a staircase, the path worn brown and notched with footholds. They come to a flat area at the top of the staircase and the younger man flops on to the grass.

'Jesus, Dad, take a break.'

'Are you serious?'

The old man is breathing normally. He stands with his back to the panorama of the city while his son gets his breath back.

'Look at that view,' says the son.

'I save it till I get to the top. Then I take it all in.'

'You're some machine. How do you keep so fit?'

'I walk a lot. I've done this climb since you were small.'

'Think I don't remember. The tears and the sore legs and the nettle stings.'

The old man smiles.

'Roy, I'm not as fit as I look. There's bits of the system not in full working order.'

'Like what?'

'When I put too much pressure on the legs I tend to blow off,' he laughs. 'Like a horse at the trot.'

The son gets to his feet.

'In that case, if you don't mind, I'll go first.'

Roy leads the way up the next section, his father speaking to him from behind.

'There's a design fault built into Man.'

'What's that?'

'Age. The teeth are beginning to go.'

'At seventy-five I'm not surprised.'

'Loosening. I've lost two big, back molars on both sides. That means their opposite numbers overgrow. Nothing to grind against. So they get sensitive. I can't eat ice-cream – or lollipops.'

The son laughs, 'I've never seen you eat an ice-cream in your life.'

'You haven't been around much lately.'

'Who's fault was that?'

The path widens and they are able to walk side by side. There is silence for a while except for Roy's breathing and the slithering noises his anorak makes with each step. The old man says, 'Would you not come and see her?'

'No.'

'I suppose I take your point. A lot of people don't get on with your mother. But there's nobody else I'd rather be with.'

'She has got to ask me back.'

'It's not off the ground you lick it – you're both stubborn.'

'I don't want to see her. Anyway, in twenty years she's hardly crossed my mind.'

'Liar.'

They come to the edge of a wood which covers most of the slope of the Cave Hill and sit down on a large stepped rock. The old man crosses his legs and Roy sits down at his feet. The day is bright but occasionally clouds pass in front of the sun. Shadows chase across the landscape.

'Remember the first time we met at the Ireland-Scotland

game? Afterwards I told her. I said, "I met Roy on the terraces today," and she said, "Roy who?"'

There is a long silence. Roy says, 'I like looking into a wood like that,' he jabs his hand towards it. 'The way you see in under the trees, like a colonnade. The way the birds echo.'

'I like seeing out. Being in a wood, seeing out to a field in the sun through trees.'

'You'd argue a black crow white.'

'I would — if it was.'

Roy laughs and digs into his anorak pocket and produces a camera. He opens the bellows and begins to photograph the woods again and again.

'That's a brave old-fashioned job.'

'A Leica,' says Roy with his eye to it, pressing the shutter. 'I got it in a junkshop in London. It's great for this kind of work. Feels like a favourite paintbrush.' He winds the film on with his thumb and changes the camera to the upright position. 'There's a lovely lens in it.' Roy turns and looks up at his father. From where he sits he can see the sinews taut in his neck. He raises the camera to his eye and focuses. The old man sees what he is doing and looks away into the woods.

'Don't start that nonsense.' The shutter clicks.

'Portrait of retired, famous architect on his seventy-fifth birthday.'

'Put that thing away.'

'But I've never taken any pictures of you.'

'Keep it like that.'

The old man begins to pluck moss from the rock he is sitting on and crosses his legs the other way revealing his thin white shin.

Roy closes the camera with a snap, returns it to his pocket and laughs, 'Forty-four years of age and I'm still looking up to you.' His father gives a snort. 'No, really. Even then . . . '

'When?'

'When you didn't come out on my side.'

'You must always remember that I chose your mother. I didn't choose you.'

Roy gives a sigh which is meant to be heard and stands up.

'I mean that philosophically — that you can't choose your children. It's not to say that I wouldn't have picked you. It's a bit like "Old Maid" − you pick and then see what you've got. There's the appearance of choice.'

They begin walking again, leaving the woods behind. On the open ground the birdsong changes from a blackbird to larks. The old man stops and looks up narrowing his eyes. He says, 'What's your own son doing?'

'Still at Aberdeen, so far as I know. At least he was before Christmas.'

'What's he like?'

'Aw − Damien, he's great. I'm very fond of him − yet there's no particular reason to be. As you say, you can't choose them. Every time I see him . . . he's gauche, unsure of himself, a bit brilliant − and sometimes he makes me laugh out loud.'

'An oddly Romish name for a grandson of mine. What's he studying?'

'Law. Aberdeen has a good reputation and it's what his mother wanted him to do.'

'You and I know that doesn't count for much.'

'I didn't even have the qualifications to get in.'

'You failed because you didn't work hard enough.'

'For fucksake, Dad, don't start. We're talking about twenty-five years ago.'

'Even though we're on a mountain there's no need for language. Save it for the terraces.'

'Do you not even give me credit for doing okay now?'

'I do.'

'It doesn't seem like it. I did all my studying a generation after everybody else.'

'At a London Poly.'

'Come on Dad, you make it sound like some sort of Craft School for the Less Able.'

'No-oo, you've got me wrong. I see your postcards all over the place. Supermarkets even.'

'And there's the possibility of a book.'

'Congratulations. I didn't know.'

'There's a lot to catch up on. Photographers who get books are few and far between.'

'What's it about?'

'Belfast. Belfast people. But I wrote the text myself.'

'Are you happy with it?'

'What?'

'The book?'

'The pictures – okay. The text I'm not sure of. The best one in the whole thing is from down by the Markets. A white horse rearing up in front of the knacker's yard. You only realize afterwards, in the darkroom, that you've got it all in the frame.'

'My father was a man who knew the value of education. His ambition for me was to get a job indoors.' The old man laughs and climbs in silence for a while.

'Why did you come back, Roy? And to Dublin of all places?'

'I got an offer of sharing some darkroom space there. In London the warring parties would have seen too much of each other. I suppose that's why Belfast was out, as well. With you and Mother.'

On the exposed side of the Hill the wind is fresher and blows his father's white hair about. He keeps trying to smooth it down with his hand.

Roy clears his throat and says, 'What galls me the most is you were right.'

'Hard to admit.'

'But it was for the wrong reasons. She wasn't even a good Catholic.'

'Thank God.'

'She gave the whole thing up after a couple of years in England.'

'But I bet she insisted on sending your boy to a Roman Catholic school.' Roy nods.

'It's ingrained deep in them.'

'That's a tautology. If it's ingrained it must be deep.'

'Thank you for pointing this out to me. My life will never be the same again.'

'Religion has f . . . nothing to do with it. She and I were . . . we just didn't get on – fought like weasels in a hole. You go through the whole bit, "It's best to stay together for the sake of the boy." But when it came to a boxing match I thought I'd better go.'

'Did you ever get married?'

'After the baby was born.'

'In a Roman Catholic church?'

'It's what she wanted at the time. Very, very quiet. There

were only about five of us. We went to a pub in the afternoon for our honeymoon.' Roy laughs and his father looks quizzically at him. 'We had to arrange an all-day babysitter.'

'I don't find it funny, even yet. Your mother has been known to cry if the subject is raised.'

'Come on, people who get married nowadays are the exception.'

'We're not talking about nowadays, we're talking about the mid-sixties. But that's only part of it. Your mother was more offended by . . . ' The old man pauses and begins to gesture with his hands. 'You know the way you feel about Jews?'

'I don't feel anything about Jews.'

'Well, the way most people feel about them. That's what we think of Roman Catholics. There's something spooky about them. As my father said, "Neither employ them nor play with them."'

'Doesn't leave much.'

'That's the idea,' he pauses again, then says, 'Taigs.'

'Do you know what that word means?'

'Fenians. Catholics.'

'I know *that*. But it's Gaelic — the word means poet.'

'So what?'

'We use it as a term of abuse — dirty taig — and all the time it means poet.'

'You're learning too much south of the border. And none of it's good for you.'

'We lack culture. Sashes and marches.'

'Nobody ever survived on poems. Hard work and thrift. People that speak their mind — that's a culture. I'm proud to be part of it — and so should you be.'

'You don't understand.'

'Why?'

Roy laughs. 'You're an oul bigot.'

'I'm a man who knows what's right and if that's being a bigot, then I am one.'

Roy stops walking and his father looks over his shoulder at him. Roy makes a fist and shakes it in the air.

'Catholics have too many children. Their eyes are too close together. They keep coal in the bath.'

His old man grins. 'Tell me something new.'

'Let's talk about something else. This is beginning to annoy me.'

'You're aisy annoyed.'

They walk on, saying nothing. Every so often Roy glances over his shoulder at the view but the old man strides on looking neither right nor left.

Ahead of them and slightly to their right they can see Napoleon's Nose, a cliff face dropping away for several hundred feet. Set back a little from the edge is a concrete beacon which from this distance looks like a wart on the nose. When they reach it Roy stands leaning against it, panting. It is covered in graffiti, the most prominent of which is a red 'No Surrender'. His father stands beside him shaking his head.

'Can you imagine carrying a spray can the whole way up here just to do that?'

'Shows Ulster determination, I suppose.'

His father goes over to the edge. A crow flaps across the space beneath him.

'You're high up when you can look down on the birds.'

'Careful,' says Roy. 'Don't stand so near the edge. In your condition one fart would propel you over.' Roy stands at a safe distance and takes out his camera. He snaps the pano-rama, moving a little to the right each time. The blue Lough lies like a wedge between the Holywood hills at the far side and the grey mass of the city at his feet and to his right. Spires and factory chimneys poke up in equal numbers. Soccer pitches appear as green squares with staples for goalposts.

The old man shouts over the wind. 'You could read regis-tration plates in Carnmoney on a day like that.'

'But who'd want to be in Carnmoney?'

'Good one, Roy.' He laughs and comes over to his son who is crouching, threading a new film into his camera. He clicks the back shut and takes three quick exposures of his feet, each time winding on with a flick of his thumb.

He looks up at his father and says, 'This was the place the United Irishmen took an oath to overthrow the English. They were all Prods as well.'

'History, Roy. It's not the way things are now.' He plucks up the knees of his trousers and sits down on the plinth of the beacon. 'It's never been worse.'

'The design fault here is the border.'

'What do you mean?'

'I think we should at least consider the island being one country.'

'Roy, please.' He shakes his head as if to rid himself of the idea, then goes on, 'The British Government are on the same side as the terrorists now. They're beating us with the stick *and* the bloody carrot. God knows where we'll be in ten years time.'

'I'd like to see a new slogan, SOME SURRENDER.'

'Never.'

'When Ireland score a try at Lansdowne Road, father — don't tell me you've no feeling for it.'

'Peripheral. That's all peripheral. What matters is our identity. We've been here from the sixteenth century.'

'A minute ago you dismissed history.' Roy reaches out and punches his father on the shoulder. The old man smiles. Roy says, 'History in Ireland is what the other side have done to you. People have got to stop killing each other and talk.'

'I read a good quote in Sunday's paper. Let me get it right. "For evil to flourish all that need happen . . . "'

'"Is that good men do nothing." That was Burke. We must read the same paper.'

'That's how the Civil Rights and the IRA got a foothold. The good men of Ulster sat back and did nothing.'

'Rubbish. The IRA probably say exactly the same thing.'

'What do you mean?'

'They see the Prods and the Brits as an evil force. Reagan used it as an excuse to bomb Libya. It *sounds* like a good phrase . . . but . . . good and evil are very personal — like false teeth, they don't transfer easily.'

'But there must be standards. Rules.'

'That's the Catholic way. Do you want me to get you an introduction?'

'Catch yourself on.'

His father takes out the binoculars and rests his elbows on his knees to scan the distance.

'I have to do it like this. Shaky hands.'

'Let's have a look.'

'In a minute.'

When the old man looks through the glasses his mou‚
opens. He focuses and swings farther to the right.

'They're clearing the site,' he says and passes the binoculars
to Roy.

'What's this?'

'You can see the lorries and the JCBs. Over there, towards
the Shore Road.' Roy raises the binoculars and finds where his
father is pointing.

'That was the multi-storey block they demolished? I saw it
on the News,' he says, without taking the glasses from his eyes.
'It was pretty spectacular coming down. Slow motion.
Wallop!'

'Lagan Point. It was one of mine.'

'I didn't know that.'

'There's a lot to catch up on.'

Roy lowers the binoculars.

His father smiles. 'The people that lived in it had a better
name for it. No Point.' The old man grunts and rises to his feet.
He stands with his hands joined behind his back looking down
on the city.

'I got a prize for it, too. There was a plaque on the wall at the
front door. It occurred to me to salvage it but the ironies were
too obvious.' He begins to rock backwards and forwards on his
feet. 'The other two I built are due to come down over the next
couple of years. Just as soon as they can get the people housed.'

'Jesus.'

'That's almost the complete works.'

Roy looks at his taut back and asks, 'Is it structural?'

'It's everything.' The old man lifts his shoulders, then drops
them. 'The whole idea came from Morocco or somewhere. A
steel skeleton with cladding. But nobody took into account the
Belfast climate. The continual rain got into the bolts no matter
how well they were sealed. Shortcuts were taken. At the time
we were looking for cheap housing for a lot of people. Quickly.
It seemed to be the answer.'

'I took some of the pictures for this book in Divis Flats.
They're pretty terrible – the Flats, not the pictures. Nobody
should be asked to live in such conditions.'

avis is not mine.' He leans back against the concrete and
is at the sky. 'The principle of living stacked is a perfectly
und one. Look what van der Rohe did in Chicago. And Le
Corbusier. What they hadn't reckoned with was the Belfast
working-class.'

'Bollicks, Dad. You can't shift the blame that way.'

'I suppose not. But the concept works with a different popu-
lation. Put security on the door, good maintenance and fill the
place with pensioners. Bob's your uncle.'

'That's like saying Northern Ireland would be fine without
the extremists. You must take account of what is. Would you
like to live in one?'

'We're living in sheltered housing at the moment . . . '

'Have you sold the house?'

'Three years ago.'

'God – after the matches I thought you were going back
home.' Roy shakes his head. 'That's really thrown me. I pic-
tured you going back to mother in our house. The place I
knew.' He shakes his head again. 'Why should that worry
me?'

'Best thing we ever did – to get rid of that barracks. Your
mother wasn't up to it and it was expensive to heat.'

'I can't think of you anywhere else.'

'We've moved into this sheltered place. It's fine. You get
your shopping done – if anyone takes ill you just press the
buzzer. I have a bit of a garden, my "defensible space", which
keeps me amused. If you came up I could give you some
broccoli.'

'And I'd get to meet Mother.' The old man shrugs his
shoulders again.

'I was *never* keen on talking to her. When she'd take me
into town to get shoes or something I kept thinking, "What'll
I talk about – I don't know what to say." At the age of twelve
I talked to my mother on the bus *about the weather*.
Because I felt I had to say something.'

The old man laughed a little, nodding.

'You're not the only one.'

'I remember on one of these jaunts she bought me a treat of
currant squares. When we came out of the shop I was so
delighted I swung the bag round and the weight of the things

tore through the bottom and they ended up all over the wet street.'

'Aw poor Roy!'

'If it had happened to me as a parent I'd have bought another bagful, but not Mother.'

'Maybe at the time we couldn't afford it.'

'Aw come on! She was training me in thrift.'

'No bad thing, if it was true.' The old man paused. 'Did you ever feel that about me?'

'What?'

'Having to make up things to say.'

'No. You always seemed to be busy. I had to fight to get talking to you. Listening to you with Charlie Burgess or Billy Muir I used to be amazed at the stories you could tell. Why didn't you tell them to me? All you'd talk to me about was filling the coal-scuttle and school. And just when it was getting interesting Mother would always say, "I think Roy should be in bed."'

'Why're we able to talk now?'

'God knows. I suppose . . . I don't know. There was a gap – for a long time – and it couldn't have been worse.'

'And here we are again.'

'Yeah, here we are again. But I'll forego the broccoli, if you don't mind. Broccoli as Trojan horse. Speaking of gifts . . . '

Roy puts his hand in another of his anorak pockets and takes out a small wrapped package. 'Happy birthday,' he says.

The old man is genuinely surprised.

'I was going to give it to you when we reached the top.'

'Well, we're here – so what's different?' His father begins to unpick the sellotape then gives up and tears off the wrapping paper. 'It seems like . . . after what you've just told me . . . like a kind of consolation prize.'

'Damn the bit.'

It is a silver hip-flask. He weighs it in his hand, then shakes it close to his ear listening to the tiny glugging noise.

'It's full.'

'For the terraces.'

The old man unscrews the cap and sniffs.

'Is there water in it?'

'Come on, Dad. I've been to three matches with you.'

The old man puts the flask to his mouth and tips it up. Afterwards he makes a face. Roy says, 'It's hall-marked.'

'I didn't know they could do that with whisky. Thanks, I'm delighted with this. How did you remember?'

Roy laughs.

'We made a date — after the Scotland game. You said why don't you drive to Belfast and we'll climb the Hill on my birthday.'

'That's right. Of course.' His father taps his temple. 'When's the next one?'

'Saturday three weeks. Against the English.'

'I'll be there.' He clenches his fist and shakes it at the sky. With his other hand he offers Roy the hip-flask.

'No thanks, I'll stick to the beer. I've never liked the taste of whisky.'

'That's what has you the shape you are.'

Roy rummages in his anorak and takes out a can of beer. He jerks at the ring pull. A small explosion of beer sprays over his father who jumps sideways. Roy laughs and apologizes.

'I forgot it would be all shook up.' He takes a hanky from his pocket and reaches towards his father. The old man ducks away.

'It's clean.' Roy dabs at the beads of beer. 'Wait — it's all over your tie.'

'Your mother'll accuse me of smelling like a brewery when I go in.'

'She'd be right.' Roy sits down to finish what is left of his can. 'For once.'

His father looks away in another direction.

'Would you not come back with me?'

Roy sighs and shakes his head.

'What would be the harm?'

'You're making it out to be a big thing,' says Roy. 'It's not. I'm not keen on talking to her — that's all.'

'But you might come round to it — some day?'

'Who knows?'

His father folds the torn wrapping paper and puts it in his pocket. Roy says, 'More thrift.'

'No. I'm anti-litter as well as everything else.' He takes up the binoculars again and looks towards the Lough.

'The constructive thing to get into these days is demolition.' He lowers the glasses and his head turns slowly from left to right. 'When I die bury me here for the view.' There is a long silence between them. Roy breaks it by laughing.

'Sure thing,' he says.

The two men go back the way they came.

'That's when you know your age.'

'What?' says Roy.

'When going down is harder than coming up.' Roy goes in front and offers his hand as they come down the steep, stepped part of the path. The old man ignores it and instead leans his weight on Roy's shoulder. Guiding him between two rocks the son puts his hand on his father's back and is startled to feel his shoulder-blades, the shape of butterfly wings, through the thin material of his jacket.

Across the Street

On summer evenings she used to practise the flute in front of a music-stand with the window open. She played with verve, her elbows high, her body moving to the tempo of the music. Every time she stopped she flicked her shoulder-length hair with her hand and, with a little backward-shaking motion of her head to make sure it was out of her way, she would begin again. In the pauses of her playing Mr Keogh could hear the slow hooting of pigeons.

From his window on the opposite side of the street he would sit on his favourite chair, a round-backed carver which supported his aching back, and watch her. He fitted the chair the way an egg fits an egg-cup. His fat hand would rest on the top of his blackthorn stick and when she had finished a piece he would knock its ferrule on the floor between his splayed feet in appreciation.

'The girl done well — the girl done very well,' he would say. Once Mrs O'Hagan, the landlady, had come the whole way up the stairs to see what he wanted.

'Me? Nothing. I'm just at one of my concerts.'

'You might have been having a heart attack,' she said and slammed the door. 'You'll cry wolf once too often,' he heard her shout from the landing.

If the afternoon was sunny he would come down the stairs stepping carefully sideways one at a time and sit with Mrs O'Hagan at the front doorway. The houses were terraced and each was separated from the street by a tiny area of garden just wide enough for Mr Keogh to stretch out his legs. Most of the other houses had privet hedges and a patch of mud or weeds but Mrs O'Hagan's had white iron railings and was flag-stoned. Window-boxes and a half barrel, painted white, bloomed with azalias, nasturtiums and begonias. There was also a little windmill with a doll figure of a man in a red waistcoat supposedly turning the handle every time the wind blew.

'It's a bit like the tail wagging the dog,' Mr Keogh had said, pointing his pipe at it. When he smoked in this garden Mrs O'Hagan insisted that he bring out an ashtray for his spent matches. Once he had struck a match on the cement between the bricks and she had looked at him in such a way that he knew never to attempt it again.

She always sat on a canvas chair and knitted while he used the more substantial wooden chair from the hallway. She knitted jumpers and pullovers and cardigans for the church bazaars at great speed. Mr Keogh noticed that she never looked at her hands while she was working but could keep the street and everything that moved in it in view. Sometimes he read the paper but in bright sunlight the tiny newsprint and the whiteness of the paper created such a glare that it hurt his eyes.

'There's your little concert artiste,' said Mrs O'Hagan. Mr Keogh looked up and saw the girl coming from Mrs Payne's door on the opposite side of the street. She wore a long kaftan and, putting her head down, walked quickly along the street. Away from her music-stand she seemed round-shouldered.

'She can fairly tootle,' said Mr Keogh.

'Aye, she's always in a hurry somewhere.'

After lunch, if it was not raining, Mr Keogh liked to walk the quarter mile to Queen Alexandra Gardens. He would sit on the first vacant bench inside the gate to recover his breath. One day he saw his flautist. She lay back with her face tilted and the undersides of her arms turned awkwardly out to catch the sun. Her eyes were closed. The weight of Mr Keogh descending at the far end of the seat made her look round.

'That's the weather, eh?' he said. She smiled a kind of wan

grin which stopped abruptly, then went back to her sun-bathing. A little later when he was breathing normally he said, 'You play the flute very well.'

'How do you know that?' The girl sat up and looked at him.

'I live opposite you.'

'I didn't know you could hear.'

'It's like everything else,' said Mr Keogh. 'There's not much you can do in this world without people getting to know.'

She shrugged and assumed her former position, feet thrust out, neck resting on the back of the bench. He noticed that when he moved she bounced slightly at the other end of the seat. He tried to keep still. He cleared his throat and asked, 'Are you working?'

'Does it look like it?'

In the silence that followed Mr Keogh took his pipe from his pocket and lit up. What little wind there was carried the smoke to the girl.

'What a good smell,' she said without opening her eyes. Mr Keogh smiled and puffed little clouds into the air. He closed down the silver lid and sat back. The girl jigged at the other end of the bench. She sat forward and scrabbled in her bag, produced a cigarette and lit it. She did this with the same urgency as she walked – as she played the flute.

'I used to play,' he said.

'The flute?'

'The cornet. In a band.'

'Oh.'

'A police band.'

One of the old march tunes went through his head and he began tapping his foot to it. He didn't whistle but clicked his tongue. The girl got up and walked away with short quick steps, her head down. She disappeared behind a clump of laurel bushes. Later, when he was leaving the park, he saw her sitting alone on a bench, her wrists still turned to the sun.

That evening in the twilight he watched her. She had switched on the light in her room with its massive white paper ball of a shade. She played a melody, some phrases of which reminded him of a tune he knew from County Roscommon. Often he had heard a flute played in the band hut and always was conscious of the spit and blow and breathiness of it. But now from across the street it was a pure sound, filtered by distance, melodic only. Her playing suddenly stopped and she made frantic flapping motions with her hands. She came forward, closed the window and pulled the curtains. Moths. Drawn by the light. Mr Keogh did not like them himself. If there was a moth, or worse a daddy-longlegs, in the room he could not sleep until it was dispatched with a firm rap from a rolled newspaper.

Mr Keogh groped his way from the chair to the bed and turned on his light. He toed off his shoes and flexed his feet. Slip-on shoes were the boon of his old age. For years he had made do with the kind of police boots he had worn in the force. Morning and night he had nearly burst blood vessels trying to tie and untie them. Now in the mornings he just put his socks on while lying in bed, swung his feet out and, with a little wiggling pressure, would insert them into his shoes, while his eyes stared straight ahead crinkling in a smile at the ease of it all. At one time he had been glad of the big boots, had even added steel tips to them so that they would make more noise. The last thing in the world he wanted was to confront and grapple with a surprised burglar. Give them plenty of time to run. That way nobody got hurt, especially him.

It was funny how the size of the feet never changed after a certain age. For as long as he could remember he had taken size eleven while the waistband of his trousers had doubled. His mother had made him wear shoes to school but he had preferred to take them off and hide them in the ditch until he was coming home. He did not want to be any different from the rest of the boys. When he did get home the first thing he would do would be to take the shoes off. His mother praised him for not scuffing them until she found out his trick, then she beat him with a strap for letting the family down in front of the teacher.

A thing they'd learned in the Force for an emergency birth was to ask the woman what size of shoes she took. The bigger the feet the easier the birth.

In his pyjamas he rolled on to the bed and into the depression his body had made in the down mattress. He slept, when he ever did sleep, propped on pillows because of his hernia. The doctor had said there was a gap in him somewhere but Mr Keogh had refused to allow an exploratory operation to find out where. A lump you could find, a gap was a different kettle of fish. The nearer he slept to the upright position the less it bothered him.

He turned out the bedside lamp and watched the sliver of light coming through the girl's curtains which had not been drawn exactly. Occasionally he saw her shadow fall on them as she moved around but she passed the slit of light so quickly that he could get no sense of her. She could have been naked for all he knew.

'What's that you're up to?' said Mr Keogh.

'Doily mats.'

The little man in the red waistcoat did not move, the day was so still. Mr Keogh wore a floppy straw hat to protect his baldness from the burning sun. He had had it since the days he dug a vegetable plot by the Waterworks. The cat had settled herself in the small square of shadow beneath Mrs O'Hagan's chair.

'What about the knitting needles?'

'This is crochet.'

Mr Keogh nodded and tilted his hat farther over his face. Mrs O'Hagan looked up at him, her hands still whirling.

'It's just a different way of tying knots,' she said. 'That's all knitting is when you come to think of it.'

Mr Keogh wiped the sweat from his forehead where the rim of his hat made contact.

'You look like you're melting,' said Mrs O'Hagan. He looked across at the shadowed side of the street. Up at his flautist's window. She was there for a moment. Next thing he knew she was skipping across the road towards him. There was something very different about her. It was her hair. She stopped at the gate.

'Can I have a light?' She held up her cigarette.

'Sure thing.' Mr Keogh leaned his bulk in the chair to get at his pocket and took out a box of Swan matches. She came through the gate and nodded to Mrs O'Hagan. Mr Keogh's fat fingers probed the box and some of the matches fell to the ground. The girl stooped to lift them. She struck one on the tiled path, lit her cigarette and tossed the match away. Mrs

O'Hagan followed its direction with her eyes. Mr Keogh offered her a little sprig of matches in case she should need them later but she refused them.

'You've had your hair done,' he said.

'Yes.' The girl reached up and touched it as if she couldn't believe. It was done in an Afro style, a halo frizzed out round her face. 'I need something to keep me going.' She laughed and it was the first time Mr Keogh had seen her do so. He saw too much of her gums.

'Have a seat,' said Mr Keogh. He was struggling to rise from his chair but the girl put out a hand and touched him lightly.

'I'll sit on the step.' She sat down and drew her knees up to her chin. She was wearing a loose white summer skirt which she held behind her knees to keep herself decent. She was in her bare feet and Mr Keogh noticed that they were big and tendony. It was as if they were painted brown. Her arms were also deeply tanned.

'Do you like it?'

'Yes.' Mr Keogh put his head to one side. 'It makes you look like a dandelion clock.' He inhaled and blew out in her direction saying, 'One o'clock, two o'clock.' She held her springy curled hair with both hands as if to keep it from blowing away and laughed again.

She tilted her face up to the sun and sighed, 'You certainly picked the right side of the street to live on.'

'I can never see', said Mrs O'Hagan 'why people want to smoke in heat like this. In the winter I can understand it.'

Mr Keogh took out his pipe and began to fill it from his pouch. Mrs O'Hagan looked away from him to the girl.

'What's your name, dear?'

'Una.'

Mrs O'Hagan repeated the name as if she had never heard it before. The girl raised the cigarette to her mouth and Mr Keogh noticed how closely bitten her nails were, little half moons embedded on the ends of her fingers, the skin bulbous around them.

'I'm Mrs O'Hagan and this is Mr Keogh from County Roscommon.'

'We've met.'

'So I gather.'

Mr Keogh lit his pipe with two matches held together. Just as he was about to set them on the arm of his chair Mrs O'Hagan got up and said, 'I'll get you both an ashtray.' She disappeared into the darkness of the hallway, stepping over the girl's feet.

Between puffs Mr Keogh said, 'Do you play the flute just for fun?'

She nodded.

'With anybody else?'

She shook her head.

'I used to play in a band,' he said. 'We had the best of crack. The paradiddles and the flam-paradiddles.'

'In the name of God what are they?' said Mrs O'Hagan, coming back with an ashtray, a Present from Bundoran. The girl immediately tapped the ash from her cigarette into it.

'They're part and parcel of the whole thing,' said Mr Keogh.

'I play music for the music,' Una said, 'but I can never play it well enough to please myself.' She spoke rapidly, her eyes staring, inhaling her cigarette deeply and taking little bites of the smoke as she let it out. A different girl entirely from the one he had met in the Gardens. 'If I could play as well as I want I would be overcome and then I couldn't go on.'

'We had to march *and* play at the same time. To get the notes right *and* the feet. No time for sentiment there, eh?'

'Maybe that's why I don't like brass bands,' said Una. There was a long silence. Mrs O'Hagan's hands still zigzagged around her half-made doily.

'Where are you from?'

'Tyrone-among-the-bushes. Near Omagh.' Una said it as if she was tired answering the question.

'And what are you working at?'

'I'm not. I was slung out of University two years ago and I've applied for jobs until I'm sick.'

'Would you not be far better off at home if you have no job to go to?'

The girl gave a snort as if that was the stupidest thing imaginable. She stubbed out her cigarette and turned to Mr Keogh.

'You're the first policeman I've ever talked to. It gives me a funny feeling.'

'Why?'

'I don't know.'

'It was a long time ago.'

'I just don't like cops — usually.' She smiled at him and he adjusted his sunhat so as to see her better.

'Do you — did you not find that people were very wary of you?'

'No — and maybe, yes. Most of my friends tended to be in the Force.'

'That's what I mean.'

'We tended to be outside things.'

'Like football grounds.' They both laughed.

Mrs O'Hagan rose from her chair and said, 'Cup of tea Mr Keogh?' He nodded. 'And you?'

'Yes, please.'

When Mrs O'Hagan had passed, the girl propped her bare feet high on the jamb of the door and clutched her dress to the undersides of her thighs.

'Mr Keogh from County Roscommon,' she said quietly and began to gnaw the side of her thumb-nail.

'I hated it. But then what else could I do?'

The girl shrugged and switched to gnawing her index finger.

'It's a pity you didn't come from County Mayo.'

'Why?'

'Mr Keogh from the County Mayo sounds better.'

'I wouldn't be seen dead coming from there.' He adjusted his hat to let some air in underneath, then he sighed, 'Una from Omagh.'

Mrs O'Hagan came out with a tray, lifting it exaggeratedly high to clear the girl's head as she sat on the step. They had tea and talked and Una borrowed two more matches and smoked two more cigarettes one after the other. Then she was away as quickly as she had come, skipping on her big bare feet across the hot street.

The conversation with the girl that day had disturbed him. He rarely thought of his days in the police now. Before going to bed he opened his cupboard and had a cup from the brandy bottle left over from Christmas. As a policeman he had been timid and useless. The only way he had survived was to hide behind the formulae of words they had taught him. If he got the words right, that combined with his awesome size and weight — in those days he was sixteen stones of muscle — would generally be enough to make people come quietly. But every time he arrested someone his knees would shake.

In drinking to forget he constantly remembered. He knew there were more important and awful things which had happened to him but one in particular stuck out. It was in Belfast shortly after he'd arrived. He had been called to a house where a man was threatening to commit suicide and he'd been met by a trembling neighbour.

'He's up in his room,' she said.

When he'd gone up and opened the bedroom door there was an old man, the sinews standing out on his neck, sitting naked on the bed with a cut-throat razor in one hand and his balls clutched in the other. There were pigeons perched along the iron bedstead, cooing and burbling. The place was white with birdshit, dressing-table, drawers, wardrobe.

'I'm gonna cut them off,' the old man had screamed. The window was wide open and the pigeons came and went with a clattering of wings.

'Suit yourself,' Keogh had said and had begun to move gently towards him. He had taken the razor from him and had intended to wrap him in the quilt but it was so congealed it had come off the bed stiff in the shape of a rectangle. He had taken a coat from the wardrobe, the shoulders of which were streaked with white.

Mr Keogh poured himself another cupful of brandy and wondered why that memory, more than all the others, frightened him so much.

He saw the girl Una several more times and each time she had changed. Once she was so excited and in such a hurry going to an interview for a job that she rushed past him giving the last part of the information walking backwards. The next time, in the supermarket, when he asked her about the job she barely acknowledged his presence and walked past him with a single item elongating her string bag. Her hair had lost some of its bushiness and had begun to lie on each side of a middle parting. She had cold sores on her upper lip which made her mouth look swollen and ugly. But from a distance it was not noticeable — like the spit and breathy sounds. Perhaps this was the reason she stopped playing the flute. Nevertheless Mr Keogh continued to watch her moving about her room. As winter approached it got dark earlier and she would turn on her light at about six. She did not bother to pull the curtains and Mr Keogh would sit in his chair and look across the street at her as she did her ironing or sat reading a magazine. Once she dodged into the room wearing only her underwear but by the time he had straightened up in the seat she was away. It wasn't that he wanted a peepshow, to be part of her privacy was enough. It gave him as much pleasure to watch her ironing as it did to see her half-dressed.

Then one night she did what he was doing and he worried for her. He had come into his room and without turning on his light looked across at her window. The place was in darkness. He sat down in his chair and waited. Staring in the darkness he thought he saw her shape sitting in the window and he felt his eyes were playing tricks on him. It must have been half an hour later when the shape moved away and it was her. After a minute she came back and sat again for the rest of the evening, just a pale smudge of a face staring down into the street. How many girls of nineteen years of age pass a Saturday night like this?

He drew his curtains and went to bed feeling heavier than ever before. He was wakened by what sounded like the slamming of a car door in the street. The luminous hands of his alarm clock said half past one. A blue light flashed a wedge on and off against the ceiling. He pulled himself from the hollow of his bed and bunching the waist of his pyjama trousers with one hand parted the curtains a little more with the other. An ambulance sat outside, its rear doors open. Farther down the street, a police car. A neighbour had come into the street to see what was happening. The door of Una's house was open. Mr Keogh put on his shoes and overcoat, took his stick and went down the stairs sideways one at a time as quickly as he dared. In the street he talked to the neighbour but he knew as little as himself. Their breath hung in the air like steam. Mr Keogh ventured up the pathway then into the lighted hall.

'Hello?'

'Hello?' The landlady's weak voice answered back.

'What's wrong?' Mrs Payne came into the hallway. She was in her dressing-gown holding tightly on to her elbows. Her face was white. A police officer stood by the kitchen door writing something down on his pad. She rolled her eyes up at the ceiling. Heavy footsteps thumped about making the pendant light tremble.

'The wee girl. She took a bath and . . . ' She drew her finger across one of her wrists. 'If I hadn't needed the toilet she'd have been there till the morning.' Her mouth wobbled, about to cry. She leaned against the wall for support.

'Is she dead?'

'I don't know. I'm not sure.'

The thumping from up the stairs increased and an ambulance man appeared carrying one end of a stretcher. Mr Keogh and Mrs Payne had to back out of the hallway to let them pass. Through the fanlight Mr Keogh saw the struggle the men had to get down the narrow stairs. On the stretcher between them was a roll of silver paper with Una's blonde hair frizzed out of it at the top. What they were carrying looked like some awful wedding buttonhole. The silver paper glittered in the street lights as the men angled the stretcher into the ambulance. Her face was as white as a candle. A voice crackled from a radio in the police car. Mrs Payne stood with both hands over her mouth. The doors slammed shut and the ambulance took off in silence and at speed with its blue light flashing. The police officer came out of the house and they drove off after the ambulance.

He went in to see if Mrs Payne was all right. She was trembling and crying.

'Sit down, sit down.' She sat and rubbed her eyes and nose with the sleeve of her dressing-gown. 'Is there anything I can do?'

'Mr Keogh,' she said, her voice still not steady. 'You'll have seen things like this before. Would you check the bathroom for me? I couldn't. I just couldn't face it.' And she began to cry again.

Mr Keogh climbed the stairs as if his whole body was made of lead.

Back in his room Mr Keogh sat down on the bed until his breathing returned to normal. He listened and could faintly hear Mrs O'Hagan's rhythmic snoring. He tried to toe off his shoes but without socks the soles of his feet had stuck. Grunting with effort he reached down and pushed them off. The alarm clock said ten past three. He got to his feet and poured himself a half cup of brandy and drank it quickly. He poured himself another and sat down. The ambulance men had let the bath out. He knew that the water would have looked like wine. But they hadn't taken time to clean up. Liver-coloured clots had smeared the white enamel and these Mr Keogh had hosed away with the shower attachment. The razor-blade he threw in the waste basket. Her clothes, the kaftan and blouse, had been neatly folded on the bathroom chair. Her Dr Scholls stood hen-toed beneath it. The brandy warmed him and fumed in his chest. He held his head between his hands and prayed to God that she wasn't dead. If he had ever married and had children she would have been the age of his grandchild. He drank off the second cup, closing his eyes. Whether she was dead or not, the fact remained that she didn't want to live. If it had been him, he could have understood it. Except that they would never have been able to lift him out of the bath. He snorted a kind of laugh and got off the bed to pour himself another drink. He took off his overcoat and hung it on the hook behind the door. She must have been suffering in her mind. He wondered why it had so affected him – he had seen much worse things. A mush of head after a shotgun suicide, parts of a child under a tram. He couldn't say it was because he knew her, because he didn't really. Was it guilt because he had intruded on her privacy by watching her. The brandy was beginning to make his lips numb. He rolled into his bed, propped himself up on his pillows and took the brandy in sips. It was not having the effect he wanted. Instead of consoling him he was becoming more and more depressed. He remembered her at the window with her elbows high and the mellow flute sounds coming across to his room.

'It's like everything else,' he said aloud. He turned to the clock and asked, 'What time is it?' A quarter to four. Fuck it anyway. What's the difference between a paradiddle and a flam-paradiddle? A flam? Very few of the drummers he had actually liked. They were a breed apart. Why? Why? Why did she do it? She had so much going for her.

'Jesus Christ the night,' he said and rolled out of bed. The floor seesawed beneath him and he had to hold on to the armchair. He established where the wall cupboard was, reached out and grasped the handles. He opened both doors and began to look through the contents stacked inside. He knelt down in case he fell down and allowed his eyes to explore the contents. A tea-tray and Phillips Stik-a-Sole advertisement were in the way and he threw them out. But when he pulled them some other stuff fell down with a crash.

Behind a wireless with a cloth and fretwork front he found the small black case. He took it out and skimmed a beard of dust from the top of it with his hand. He blew on it as well but the dust was stuck. He stood up and fell back on the bed. He opened the catches and lifted the lid. It was so long since he had seen it. The silver shine of it had gone — it looked dull like pot aluminium.

'Stop. Stop everything.' He lay across the bed and had another drink from the cup on his bedside table. He turned back to the cornet and picked it out of its purple plush. He hawed on it and tried to rub it with the sleeve of his pyjamas. The valves were a bit stiff, but what comfort to get his little finger into that hook. It felt right. It balanced. He raised it to his lips and only then realized that the mouthpiece wasn't fitted. Fuck it. In the purple plush there were three. He selected his favourite and slotted it into the tube. He wiggled the valves up and down with his fingers trying to free them. A march came into his head and his foot began tapping to it. He cleared his throat, thought better of it and had another drink of brandy, then raised the cornet to his lips. What came out sounded like a fart.

'Who did that?' he said and laughed. He raised the instrument again and this time it was better. He got the tune and it was loud and clear. He knew it so well he couldn't remember the name of it. He didn't tap his bare foot but stamped it up and down to the rhythm of the march. He found he was short of puff very quickly.

'What else?' he said. Occasionally they used to have jazz sessions after band practice and Brian Goodall would sing. He began to play, hearing the voice, knowing the words. His foot stamped to the slow beat and his heel hurt and the notes, now harsh, rang out.

With a crash his bedroom door burst open and Mrs O'Hagan stood there in her nightdress.

'In the name of God Mr Keogh what are you up to?' He smiled and turned slowly to face her.

'A late hour,' he said and laughed.

'Do you know what time it is? Some of us have to be up for Mass in the morning.'

'Sorry. But that wee girl across the street . . . ' It came out slurred. Mrs O'Hagan sniffed the air and looked at the almost empty brandy bottle.

'If this ever happens again, Mr Keogh, you can find yourself another place to live.' She slammed the door as hard as she could.

'The boy done bad — the boy done very bad,' he said and rolled over on to the bed. He fell asleep almost immediately.

At midday he woke up with his head pounding and the track of the cornet, like a relief map of his innards, exact even to the gap, imprinted in his side where he had slept on it.